SIREN
Publishing

Everlasting Classic

A Home
for
Three
Marla
Monroe

Lost in Space 3

A Home for Three

Andrea's attraction to Coreg has PJ wondering if he's willing to share. He only wants her to be happy and is willing to do just about anything to make that happen. Does that include accepting Coreg into their life? If that is what it takes to be a family, PJ will welcome the other man.

Andrea is familiar with PJ and comfortable with him as her man. Her attraction to Coreg is sudden and scary. He brings her back her beloved sewing machine from the wreckage of their ship so is it gratitude or is she already half way in love with this strange alien?

Coreg knows that Andrea is the female for him. He sees something in her that warms his soul when he never thought he'd have a female of his own. Sharing her with the human male isn't an issue for him. He'll do anything to be a part of her life, including working with the human to make her happy.

Genre: Ménage a Trois/Quatre, Science-Fiction
Length: 34,899 words

A HOME FOR THREE

Lost in Space 3

Marla Monroe

Siren Publishing, Inc.
www.SirenPublishing.com

ABOUT THE AUTHOR

Marla Monroe has been writing professionally for over thirteen years. Her first book with Siren was published in January of 2011, and she now has over 75 books available with them. She loves to write and spends every spare minute either at the keyboard or reading. She writes everything from sizzling-hot cowboys, emotionally charged BDSM, and dangerously addictive shifters, to science fiction ménages with the occasional badass biker thrown in for good measure.

Marla lives in the southern US and works full-time at a busy hospital. When not writing, she loves to travel, spend time with her feline muses, and read. Although she misses her cross-stitch and putting together puzzles, she is much happier writing fantasy worlds where she can make everyone's dreams come true. She's always eager to try something new and thoroughly enjoys the research she does for her books. She loves to hear from readers about what they are looking for in their reading adventures.

You can reach Marla at themarlamonroe@yahoo.com, or
Visit her website at www.marlamonroe.com
Her blog: www.themarlamonroe.blogspot.com
Twitter: @MarlaMonroe1
Facebook: www.facebook.com/marla.monroe.7
Google+: https://plus.google.com/u/0/+marlamonroe7/posts
Goodreads:
https://www.goodreads.com/author/show/4562866.Marla_Monroe
Pinterest: http://www.pinterest.com/marlamonroe/
BookStrand: http://bit.ly/MzcA6I
    Amazon page: http://amzn.to/1euRooO

For all titles by Marla Monroe, please visit
www.bookstrand.com/marla-monroe

A HOME FOR THREE

Lost in Space 3

MARLA MONROE
Copyright © 2018

Chapter One

"Watch out."

Andrea Pickens stepped back on the walkway just as a transport scooted around the corner where she'd been standing. She'd been so in awe of the lovely buildings, she wasn't paying attention to where she'd been walking.

An enormous Levassisan loomed over her as she wobbled on the walkway after the transport had passed. He had to be nearly seven feet tall and was built like a linebacker from Earth's football sports.

"Are you okay? Were you injured?" His silver eyes and nearly white hair startled her.

If she lived there the rest of her life she would never get used to their metallic colors and nearly matching hair. Like all Levassisans, this one wore his hair braided down his back.

"I'm fine. Thank you for the warning. I wasn't paying attention."

"You shouldn't be out on your own. You could get hurt."

"I'm usually not so scatterbrained, but your homes are so beautiful that I forget myself." She stuck out her hand. "I'm Andrea. Thank you again."

"I'm called Coreg. It is my pleasure to make your acquaintance. Please allow me to see you back to your home. Who is your protector?"

It wasn't lost on her that he didn't shake her hand. She'd forgotten how formal they were there.

"I don't have a protector. I don't need one." Andrea shook her head. "I don't think I'll ever get used to this way of life. You assure us that no one would harm us here, yet you feel that we need someone to watch over us. I don't get it."

"No one would willingly harm you, but many of our males are anxious for a female and might approach you to convince you to accept them as your male. It is safer for you to always be in the company of a protector when you're out in the city." Coreg offered his arm. "Where did you want to go? I will escort you."

"Thank you, but I don't need an escort. I was just exploring. I wanted to see some of the shops and just get an overall look at the city."

"Then I will be your protector while you are doing that. Allow me to show you our home." He waited until Andrea finally laid her hand on his forearm.

"First, I'll take you to the street where all of our major shopping is done. Have you been to the city's center where most Levassisans eat and commune?"

"Yes. I've been there several times with friends."

"I trust that there was a male to escort you when you went," he said.

"Well, yes. I guess there was. Several of our men went with us."

"And are any of these males your males?" he asked.

"My males? Oh, you mean am I married to any of them. No. There is one that is special to me though, PJ. He's fun and easy going. I like him. He was one of the men I was supposed to be with when we were going to the second planet to live."

"PJ, that is an odd name. Those are initials if I am interpreting them correctly. Why is he not with you?"

"His real name is Peter James but everyone calls him PJ. He's working in one of your facilities helping with maintenance or something."

"Who is the other male of your family unit?"

"There isn't one. He died during the crash. I hate that he died, but I didn't really know him." Andrea shrugged.

"I'm sorry you lost the other part of your unit. Have you chosen another?" he asked.

Andrea wasn't sure why he was so interested, but it made her uncomfortable. She changed the subject.

"Is it true that you don't use money here?" she asked.

"That is correct. We barter for things we want but for the things we really need, they are free for our use. Everyone here works for the common good of the whole. It is our way."

"It seems so simple, but it would never have worked on Earth."

"It is simple, and it does work here."

Coreg led her to a shop that held yards of lovely fabrics. She ooed and ahhed over the pretty floral colors and sturdy samples that had to be more for workers than for a woman. It made her wonder who wore the pretty colors.

"If there are so few women here, why are there so many nice colors and prints?" she asked.

"Many of our leaders wear the brighter colors as a sign of their station. Also, now that there are females here in Levastah, they are displaying more of them for you to choose from. We're all hoping you'll adapt to them and enjoy their superior workmanship." Coreg held up a bright yellow next to her face. "This would look amazing on you with your sun-kissed skin."

Andrea could feel heat travel up her neck into her cheeks. He was flirting with her. She wasn't sure how to react.

I didn't know they knew how to flirt. Usually they seem so stoic and stern.

"It is lovely, but I don't have any way to make clothes from it," she told him.

"You wouldn't need to. Our clothers will create a lovely dress for you. If you like this, we can ask them to make you one."

"I don't have anything to barter or a way pay for it. No one will let me work."

"Females do not work. They are cared for and protected." Now he was back to the stern Levassisan she'd begun to get used to.

"Would they let me make my own dress? I love to sew. I just don't have a sewing machine. It's back on the ship."

Coreg cocked his head to one side. "You are saying that you brought a machine that you make dresses with you on the ship that crashed? Why would you wish to make your own clothes?"

"Because it makes me happy. I like creating new things. I would love to be able to make dresses and other clothes for the other women here." Andrea looked up with what she hoped were pleading eyes.

He looked down at her with his silver gaze and drew in a deep breath that he let out in a long sigh. She hoped it meant he was going to ask if she could use their sewing machine.

"I do not think this is a good idea, but I will ask for you. If it is something you really want to do. I want you to be happy here." Coreg cornered the clerk and talked with him for several long moments.

When he returned to her, it was with a frown pulling at his already stern features. She could tell he wasn't happy with whatever the outcome of the conversation had been.

"The storekeeper isn't pleased, but he will allow you to approach his colleague who does the sewing here to see if he will allow you to use his machine. I don't think it will be what you expect though." Coreg held out his arm once more and they walked to the back of the building and down a short hall before he opened a door to the left.

Inside was a room awash in color. Brightly colored draperies hung all around the room with a strange machine off to one side. Nothing in the large room looked the least like one of her sewing machines. It disappointed her. She wouldn't enjoy using the big thing that they used to create clothes. She sighed and took a step back.

"What is it, Andrea? Is something wrong?" Coreg laid a tentative hand at her back before just as quickly removing it.

"Their machine that makes clothes is nothing like my machine. I wouldn't be able to use it, and I don't think I'd even like using it," she said.

"Is there something I can do for you?" the tall, darkly bronze male asked.

"No, not right now. She wished to see how you made the clothes you've made for her and her friends." Coreg steered her out of the room and back down the hall.

Sadness had her frowning as they walked outside again. She no longer felt like exploring the beautiful city. She might as well return to the home where she, PJ, and Lettie were living. Andrea looked up at the beautiful male.

"I'm ready to go home now. I don't feel like exploring any longer."

"Did I say something wrong, Andrea? I wouldn't hurt or anger you for any reason." Alarm had his eyes flashing silver and his face pulled down into a frown. She hated seeing that look on his amazing face, but she didn't want to go anywhere else. All her hopes had been dashed.

"No, you didn't do or say anything wrong. I just don't feel like going anywhere else. I'd been hoping to find somewhere that I could get material and a machine to make dresses and blouses for us," she told him.

"The males at that shop and other shops in our city would be glad to make whatever you want, Andrea. Why would you want to create your own?"

She didn't know how to explain it to him. It wasn't something he could understand when they didn't allow women to work and catered to them instead of supporting their need to contribute.

"Sewing is something I do that makes me feel good. It's like whatever you do making you feel good." Andrea looked up at him. "What do you do?"

"I'm an overseer for the crops in my area. Today is my day of rest."

"And I was dragging you around when you probably had somewhere you wanted to be. I'm sorry. I'll just return to my house and let you continue on." Andrea turned around and headed back the way she'd come.

"Wait, Andrea. Allow me to escort you back. You shouldn't be alone. What if you wander off the walkway again and are injured? It would be my honor to see to your safety." Coreg held out his arm expectantly.

What can it hurt? It seems to make him happy to take me back. I'll let him lead me then he can return to whatever he'd had planned before I sidetracked him.

Andrea took his arm and allowed him to see her back to the house. When they arrived, Lettie ran outside to greet them.

"Did you find a machine? Will you make me some clothes as well?" Lettie barely stopped for air.

"They don't have machines like I use. I'd never be able to make anything using them. We'll have to let them keep making these tunics for us," Andrea told the other woman.

"Can't we go back to the ship and find yours?" she asked.

"PJ says it's too dangerous. He said even if we did, it would probably be busted."

"Maybe not." Lettie didn't seem to want to let it go. "I love those dresses you showed us when we were on the way to the planet. I was so looking forward to some of them." Lettie sighed.

"Perhaps you could show me what it looks like, and I can convince our leaders to allow me to go back and look for it for you." Coreg's stern features had relaxed slightly.

"You'd do that?" Andrea asked, almost afraid to get her hopes up once again.

"Yes. If it would make you happy, I would be honored to search for this machine you are talking about."

"I'll draw you a picture of what it looks like. Come inside with us."

"I will return tomorrow to obtain this picture. It isn't permitted for a male to enter another male's home when there are females in residence without that male being present." He turned to leave.

Andrea stopped him with a hand on his arm. "You'll come back?"

His face relaxed further. "I will return tomorrow after my shift in the fields. If the machine is not damaged, I will bring it to you once I discuss it with the leaders of our planet."

"Do you think they will let you go out to get it?" she asked.

"If it will make a female happy, I think there is a good chance they will agree to it." Coreg reached out and touched Andrea on the cheek in a light caress. "I will convince them for you, Andrea."

Long after he'd left, Andrea could feel his touch there. It worried her. She and PJ were already linked together from when she'd been placed on the ship to another planet. Landon hadn't made it, but that didn't mean she didn't plan to be with PJ. They were taking it slow since everything was so new to all of them. She really liked the man, and knew she could easily fall in love with him.

Where did that leave her with the budding feelings she'd already begun to develop for Coreg? And why had it happened so fast?

Coreg was charming and easy to talk to. She couldn't help but be physically attracted to him. He was a beautiful man. His muscular frame could easily handle her plus-sized curves, and she thought that even PJ would like him.

Thinking of PJ made her wince. He wouldn't be pleased when he met Coreg. He thought they were going to be together and hadn't expected that she'd want a second man in their relationship after losing Landon.

Andrea sighed. Did she want a second man in their relationship? Why? Wasn't she happy with PJ? She was. Deep in her heart she was happy with him and wanted to be with him, but something had latched on to Coreg, and she wanted to know what it was and what it meant for all of them.

Chapter Two

Coreg sighed. He liked the pretty female with her dark looks. All that dark black hair that reminded him of the darkest of nights and those dark eyes that lit up when she smiled. A male would do much to see that smile on her face. He was already to that point. He'd agreed to approach their leaders to ask that he and a few males make the trip back to the crashed ship to look for the female's sewing machine.

He knew it might end up being a futile search, but Coreg would still ask. He had the drawing of the machine and the area in which it would have been housed. They would also bring back anything more that might be of need to the humans. It was one of the things that might appeal to the leaders to allow such a trip.

"Coreg, you have audience with our council. You may enter now." The guard at the door to their chambers opened the door to allow him entrance.

He approached the males and bowed his head to them. They were mostly made up of the elders of their race who were wise beyond their years, and who saw to the health, happiness, and general safety of their planet.

"Coreg. What do you wish to ask of the council?"

"I would like to lead a small team back to the crashed spaceship of the humans. One of the females is a seamstress and wishes for her machine so that she can make clothes for her friends. When I pointed out that we have those here who can make whatever she wants, she saddened and said that sewing made her happy. I wish to see this female happy."

"She likes to work making clothes for others?" one of the council males asked, his face mirroring his obvious confusion.

"Yes. She enjoys creating things and said it was what made her happiest when on the spaceship."

"You are hoping to join with this female?" Another council member asked.

"It is too soon to know, but yes. I would like her to be my female. She already has a human male she is bonded to, but since it has been agreed that there should be two males to each female, I'm hoping they will allow me to join with them."

The males on the council all conversed among themselves. After a few moments, the council's leader spoke up.

"Why can't she use the machines we have here?"

"They are far too large and different from what she is used to. She said she'd never understand them and they wouldn't give her the happiness that her own machine can give her. I must admit that the machine she had described and drawn on paper looks nothing like ours. It is much smaller."

"Then we will allow you and four others to make this trip. You can also bring back anything you believe the humans would value to help them better assimilate into our culture."

Coreg couldn't stop the smile that their words gave him. He bowed and backed out of the room. Next, he had to pick some males to go with him. One had to be a soldier with experience fighting the Aragus, a creature that was nearly impossible to kill with its hardened skin and ability to scamper off on four legs. It was deadly to most Levassians. He planned to leave early at the sun's rise.

Since the eros scourge, there were only a handful of females left on Levasso. It had killed most of the females and many of their males. Now the few who were left were sequestered with their males and very old. They'd looked for females who were compatible for many years, but had just about given up, believing their race would die out.

With the crash of the Earth ship, they had new hope. There had been many females who they hoped would mate with Levassians, producing young. Already, Veran, Gressen, and Sabin had mated with human females and young were expected within the year. Everyone was patiently waiting their births. No one much cared what they looked like as long as they were healthy.

Corag wanted a mate and young of his own. He would pursue the beautiful female and hopefully convince her and her partner, this PJ, to accept him as their third. To be a part of a family unit, Coreg was willing to do most anything.

So early the next morning, almost before the sun had risen, he and four other males took a transport as far as they were able, then guided small hover carts the rest of the way. They would be able to haul most anything using the carts. He hoped they'd find Andrea's sewing machine to bring back. Even if it was damaged, he would return it in hopes that one of their craftsmen could repair it with her guidance.

Once they arrived at the craft, he noted how the vegetation had already begun to claim the massive ship. If it wasn't for the dangers outside the city walls, they would have long since harvested whatever they could from the craft, but it was dangerous in the jungles of Levasso. Many animals roamed the unguarded area. They'd had no need to expand and tame some of the area since they had few left in their home.

The five males entered the cargo area of the ship where they'd first found the human survivors. He began searching among the cargo bins for the numbers to the carton that held Andrea's machine. The other males opened crates that hadn't been opened before and stacked as much of the cargo as they could onto the hover carts while Coreg continued his search.

After nearly an hour, he found the bin that held Andrea's things. He popped open the lid and found the box-like contraption that housed her sewing machine. The decal of human clothes alerted him to the machine right away. He hauled it out and placed it on the hover cart he'd claimed as his, then gathered the other boxes she'd asked for. Then he looked for other things that he thought would please the other humans.

"We've filled our carts, Coreg. Are you ready to return?" one of the others asked.

"Yes. I've found what I came for. It is a good trip. Let's return to the city now."

The entire trip back, while he thought about Andrea and her beauty, the soldier kept a constant vigil for dangers that lurked in the trees. Coreg should have been more diligent, but he was too excited to pay much attention. Luckily, they made it back to the transport without trouble. They loaded the carts onto it and hurried back into the city.

Coreg couldn't wait to return to Andrea and see her face when she realized he'd brought back her sewing machine. The thought of her face lighting up made his dick hard.

He'd just pulled up in the small transport when Andrea and Lettie burst out of the door of the house, followed by a strong looking human male with light colored hair of brown and red. He stood about six feet two inches and had light brown eyes. At this moment, those eyes looked cautious as he moved between him and the two females.

"Did you find it?" Andrea asked, wringing her hands.

"I did. It looks to be unharmed as were the cartons it came in. I will carry it inside for you." He stepped off the transport and picked up the sewing machine.

"I can handle it." The human male stepped forward to take the machine.

"I would be most grateful if you'd carry in some of the other things she asked for," he said, moving to one side to avoid the male.

"Coreg, this is PJ. He's um, my male. You've already met Lettie." Andrea indicated the human male standing just in front of her.

"It is an honor to meet Andrea's male." Coreg nodded at him.

"Thank you for bringing back her sewing machine and supplies. She's been pretty depressed over not having them. I would have gone to get them but no one would let me, saying it was too dangerous."

"It is very dangerous, but I took a soldier and three others with me to obtain her things. I wished to see her happy and the pretty smile back on her face." Coreg hoped he could convince the male to allow him to court his female.

PJ sighed. "Come on in. I have to admit that Andrea has been really excited that she might get her machine back. Thanks for getting it for her."

Coreg let out a quick breath. He was inside at least. That was a start."

* * * *

PJ watched the tall, silver-toned man carry the box sewing machine case into the house as if it weighed nothing. He picked up two of the boxes off the transport and followed him and the women inside where they set down their boxes, then returned outside to bring in the remainder of the boxes.

"Thank you for allowing me to help with carrying these inside. I realize you are Andrea's male and don't have to allow me entrance," the big man said.

"Andrea likes you and you did make her happy by bringing her that damn machine. I would have gotten it for her if they'd have let me."

"I'm sure you would have. A good male will do anything to make his female happy."

Yeah, I will.

PJ drew in a deep breath and let it out. "I get the feeling you're wanting more than just to see Andrea smile."

Coreg stopped just outside the door to the home they'd been given for their use. "It is probably too soon, but I'd like to approach Andrea and you about being the third in your family unit. I would work hard to make her happy and help you in any way to make sure she is."

He looked up then back down at the boxes he was carrying. He'd been right. Coreg wanted his Andrea. He couldn't blame the big man. She was lovely and sweet. Plus, she was a female and the men of Levasso would do just about anything to capture the heart of one of their women. They were all a little desperate.

"I'm sure you would. You've gone a long way to capturing her heart already. If she's really interested, I'll think about it. I just want her happy and we were already supposed to form ménage relationships before we crashed, but I don't know you like I knew our third that died. If you push, I'll push back." PJ watched the other man's face for his reaction, but he only nodded.

"I understand. Andrea's happiness is as important to you as it is to me. I will not push, as you say."

PJ followed Coreg inside where they set the remainder of the boxes on the floor in the large communal living area. Andrea and Lettie were looking over the machine, which she'd set up on the table in the living space.

"Is it okay?" PJ asked.

Andrea looked up with a broad smile on her face. "It's perfect. We're just threading it and getting it oiled up. I can't wait to start sewing. Maybe we can go back to that shop Coreg took me to and get some of the pretty material."

PJ nodded. "No problem. We'll go tomorrow. I'm off tomorrow."

"That's fine. I have plenty in these boxes to get started on. I want to make Lettie a pretty dress so she can impress Tegrig and his brother at the communal food court."

"Andrea. They aren't interested in me. They were just being nice talking with us the other night."

"I am sure that any male would be interested in your beauty, Lettie. They would be a fool not to be," Coreg said.

Lettie's sweet face reddened as she looked away. PJ liked the Levassian more for his kindness to the young woman. She'd been so young to have ended up on a spaceship bound for another planet, and expected to take on two men. He could tell that Andrea had latched on to her in an effort to alleviate some of the poor woman's fears. It was one of the reasons he cared so deeply for Andrea. Could he share her with the Levassian? Coreg seemed nice enough.

I'm going to have to face it sooner or later. It was decided when we were taken in by the inhabitants here that every human female would take at least two males whether they were Levassian or human. I was going to have to share her regardless. Coreg isn't all that bad.

At least he seemed straightforward so far. PJ would wait to cast his vote until he learned more about the man. Andrea would be the one to make the final decision, but he was sure she would consider how he felt on the subject when she did.

"Perhaps you would allow me to accompany you all when you return to the commune for last meal next?" Coreg asked.

Andrea's quick smile told PJ that she was pleased that the man had asked. She looked over at him.

"If Andrea and Lettie would like that, I'm fine with it," he finally said.

"Do come," Andrea said as her mouth blossomed into a wide smile.

PJ's heart skipped a beat like it always did when she did that. His cock reacted as well by stiffening in his jeans. He wanted to adjust it but didn't want to draw attention to it.

"I would be honored to attend with you. When do you plan to go again?" Coreg asked.

Andrea looked over at PJ with a questioning look.

"We thought to go the day after tomorrow. Andrea and Lettie has cooked several meals of late that we are finishing up," he told him.

"I will arrive after my shift and walk with you," Coreg said. "I should leave now and allow you to rest and have your meal. Thank you again for allowing me to attend with you."

PJ walked the man out, offering his hand to shake. To his surprise, Coreg took it and shook it, though they rarely did that. He could tell that the man was trying to gain PJ's support. He'd reserve judgement until he had spent more time around the man.

PJ watched Coreg return to the transport, then pull away from the house to disappear down the clean sparkling streets. When he returned to the living area it was to find the women had abandoned the machine and the communal living area. He located them in the meal prep room.

"I'm sure you're hungry. You've been working all day. Food should be ready in about fifteen minutes, PJ," Andrea said.

"No hurry. You like this Coreg, don't you?" he said.

Her face turned a light shade of pink as she busied herself at the sink. "Yeah. He's nice. He went out of his way to get my sewing machine."

"He did. You know he likes you and wants to be one of your men."

"I know. It's too soon to think about that, but I do like him. He's kind and treated Lettie here just as well as he treated me."

Lettie's face heated again as if the man had just paid another compliment to her. PJ thought she was the cutest thing but much too young for him. They'd need to watch out that she ended up with men who would treat her carefully.

"He seems pretty nice. I'm glad he was able to find your machine. I know how much you love to sew. It won't be long until you'll be making clothes for everyone here if you're not careful. I saw some of the things you'd made back on the ship. They were amazing," he told her.

"Thanks. I've always loved to sew. My grandmother taught me before she died. I was only seventeen," she told him.

"Did your mother sew?" he asked, desperate to learn all he could about her.

"No." Andrea laughed. "Granny said she was too impatient and couldn't sit still as a child. She liked to garden and spend time outside with her dad."

"Did you enjoy gardening?" he asked.

"Some, but not like my mom."

"What about your brother? Did he like spending time outside?"

"Mike was just like my mom. He'd rather be outside hunting or fishing than anywhere else. He and Dad used to go hunting or fishing almost every weekend. Mom would mess around in the yard or garden, and Granny and I would sew." Andrea's eyes grew distant as if she were remembering those times.

"I'm glad he got to go on one of the ships. You know he's out there somewhere making a new life," PJ told her.

She laughed. "And doing what he loves to do most. Hunting and working outside."

"Do you think you can be happy here, Andrea?" PJ asked.

"I already am, PJ. I have you and Lettie, and now my sewing machine."

It was more than he'd hoped for. She'd included him in one of the things that made her happy.

Chapter Three

Andrea hummed as she cut out the pattern for the dress she was making Lettie. She wanted to have it ready by the next night. The initial piecing it together wouldn't take long, she'd fit it to the other woman's body then sew it up so that it fit her perfectly. She loved seeing a finished garment on the person she'd created it for. It gave her a sense of accomplishment and pride.

"It's so hard to believe that you're going to make one of those beautiful dresses out of those pieces of material. I can't even see how they go together," Lettie said.

The other woman had been watching her all morning from the couch. She'd been like a giddy teenager when Andrea had measured her and written down everything to use when she put the dress pieces together.

"I can't wait to try it on."

"Just remember that you have to be careful in it when it's just pinned together. You could stick yourself or rip the material," Andrea cautioned.

"I will." She stood up. "I'm going to go sit outside and enjoy the fresh air while it's not so hot out. Once the suns get directly overhead it's too hot to do anything."

Andrea smiled as Lettie walked across the room and opened the door. The bright light from outside could be blinding if you weren't careful to keep your eyes averted. She'd have to check on the other woman in a little while to be sure she didn't fall asleep sitting under the outside covering and overheat.

She'd noticed that if they spent any time out in the heat of the suns they got tired much faster and had to drink copious amounts of water to keep from dehydrating. She'd limited her time outside to early morning or late afternoons when the suns were nearly behind the distant mountains or the dense jungles. It severely limited the time any of them could travel around the city.

Once she'd pieced together the dress with pins, Andrea stood up and stretched. She started toward the door when Lettie walked inside fanning her face.

"It's so hot out there. I'm going to fix some of that flavored drink they have. Do you want a glass?" she asked.

"Please. When you finish and have cooled off, I'm ready for you to try on the dress. It's just pinned together, mind you, but you'll see what it's going to look like." Andrea couldn't help but smile at the excited brightness in Lettie's light blue eyes.

"Will it be ready in time to wear to the community meal tomorrow night?" she asked.

Andrea nodded. "I'll have it ready. It won't take all that long to sew it together. The most time-consuming part will be hemming it. I do that by hand so that the stitches don't show."

"I can't wait. Everyone will be so jealous that I have a human dress to wear while they're all having to wear those tunic dresses they made for us," Lettie said.

The girl's face pinched up in distaste. None of the human women liked the long flowing gowns that resembled tents to them. They were overly modest and cumbersome. She had to admit that they tended to keep them cooler when they were outside, but were uncomfortable to walk around in.

"Maybe you can start a business and sew for everyone," Lettie suggested.

"I don't mind making clothes. Since they don't use money here, I won't even have to charge for doing it. They just need to bring me the material and tell me what they want." Andrea could see herself staying busy and loving it. As long as she didn't feel pressed to get something made because someone was paying for it, she'd enjoy it.

"I hadn't thought about that. Do you mind sewing if you aren't getting paid?" Lettie asked.

"No. I'll like it even more if I don't have to worry about charging and collecting money." She smiled at the other woman and accepted the glass of flavored water from her. "Sit down and cool off so you can try on the dress."

While she fitted and adjusted the pinned garment on Lettie, Andrea thought about Coreg and the fact that he was going to go with them to the meal the next night. She really liked him and had thought about him a good bit all morning. She was glad that PJ wasn't upset that she'd developed an interest in the Levassian. He could have been irate over it, but instead, he was reserving judgement until they'd spent time around the man.

Andrea's body reacted to her thoughts about his silver skin and those bright silver eyes. She squeezed her legs together, embarrassed that she'd grown wet just thinking about him. Why had she become so attracted to him after only a chance meeting? It didn't make sense, but she had. She could easily see him with her and PJ, writhing on the bed together. Her pussy contracted at the thought.

"Andrea? Are you okay? Your face is all flushed. Have you gotten too hot working on the dress?" Lettie's voice lifted in alarm.

"I'm fine. I think I'll have another glass of this water before I start sewing." She stood up and walked into the other room trying to think about something else so she'd calm down.

Andrea fanned her face then poured another glass from the cold box as they called the fridge. After a few minutes, she felt calm enough to return to the living room to begin sewing on the dress. Lettie was dozing on the couch, a pamphlet lying open on her abdomen as if she'd fallen asleep reading.

She woke Lettie up a little while later to eat the mid-day meal then she resumed work on the dress while Lettie cleaned up in the kitchen.

By the time PJ returned from working, she'd started hemming the dress. It would take several hours to make the minute stitches around the circumference of the dress, but she was sure she'd have it ready for Lettie to wear the next night.

"How was work?" she asked PJ when he'd stripped off his coveralls and stepped out of the boots he wore for the job.

"Good. We've been able to help them repair some of the machinery they use for irrigating their crops. They'd abandoned some of it because no one knew how to fix it. Some of their talents have died off with the men who'd created them. Since they don't have younger men to learn from the older ones, a lot of their history is being lost."

"That's sad. I guess we are a godsend for them. Not only because we're women, but also because you all can help with the other things. I just wish that they'd let women who wanted to work do so," she said.

"Della and Caro have managed to lift some of the restrictions for that, but it will take time before they will make sweeping changes. With them pregnant now, they are pretty much sequestered until they have their babies," PJ told her.

"I know they are a big deal for everyone," she said.

"You have no idea how excited the Levassians are about their pregnancy. They haven't had children here for years and years. They can't wait to welcome them to the world. I hear they are planning a huge celebration for each child's birth, and are creating toys for them to play with as they grow up."

"That's so sweet. I bet they'll have hundreds of doting uncles to spoil them rotten."

Andrea thought about having children and realized that for the first time, she was excited about the idea. Where before she'd been a little apprehensive about it since they'd been charged with having as many children as possible when they'd left Earth, now she looked forward to it.

"Meal's ready if you guys are ready to eat." Lettie's cheerful voice pulled her back from her thoughts.

"Looks like you've just about finished Lettie's dress." PJ walked ahead of her to the meal prep room.

"All that's left is the hemming. I'll be working on that all day tomorrow. I won't do much more tonight. I'm kind of tired. It's been awhile since I've cut out patterns and put them together."

"Oh, Andrea. I'm sorry. I didn't mean to rush you." Lettie's face fell.

"No. Don't be sorry. I've thoroughly enjoyed it. You haven't rushed me. I'm just looking forward to relaxing some before bed. That's all." Andrea hated that she'd taken some of the excitement away from the woman.

"If you can't finish it tomorrow, it's not a big deal, Andrea," Lettie insisted.

"It won't take much longer to have it hemmed, Lettie. Don't worry about it. I'm not pressured. This is what I love to do."

"If you're sure."

PJ chuckled. "Believe me, Lettie. All she talked about on the spaceship was how much she was looking forward to sewing once we got where we were going. You should have known her then."

* * * *

The next night, Andrea watched as Lettie twirled around in her new dress giggling and laughing as she looked in the mirrored wall that only took a touch to turn it from the light blue to a mirror. The young woman looked beautiful in the green dress with orange trim. It suited her tanned skin and blonde good looks.

"You look amazing, Lettie. Tegrig and Honrig will be stunned. I bet they won't be able to say a word when they see you," Andrea said.

"Hurry up, ladies. Coreg will be here soon, and I want to see what Lettie looks like," PJ called through the door.

"Come on. We better get out there before PJ has a coronary." Andrea touched the mirror and it turned back into a wall.

"I'm so excited." Lettie pressed the spot that opened the door of the bedroom.

"Wow. You look pretty as a picture, Lettie." PJ smiled at the young woman.

"Thanks." She giggled then hurried down the hall toward the living area.

"You look nice, too. I like that shade of pink on you, babe." PJ reached out and touched her chin.

"Thanks. I did some alterations to the tunic they made for us. It was just too billowy for me," Andrea said.

"It looks nice," he said.

"I think I can salvage a lot of what they made for us since the dresses are so large, and remake them into smaller, better fitting outfits. I'm going to experiment on mine some next week."

"Just don't overdo it, Andrea. Remember that you get tired faster here," PJ reminded her.

"I know. I'll rest. Lettie is the one who needs to be more careful. I've had to warn her not to sit outside too much several times. She loves being outdoors, but I'm afraid she's going to get too hot."

"Maybe having these Tegrig and Honrig fellows interested in her will help with that. They may want to spend time with her and will watch out for her if they do. These guys are very protective of you women," he said.

"I know. Coreg was horrified that I'd gone walking into town the other morning. It was early and I knew better than to stay out in the sun too long, but he didn't think I should have been out alone at all."

"Like I said, overprotective. Still, it was probably a good thing he watched out for you. I've heard that some of the men here are getting bothersome to some of the women. They're desperate for a woman of their own."

"That's so sad. I can't imagine what it must feel like to see something you might not ever get to have."

"True. I guess I hadn't thought about it like that." PJ took Andrea's elbow and escorted her down the hall to the living area just as there was a knock at the door. "I bet that's Coreg."

"I've got it." Lettie bounced to the door and opened it with a broad smile. "Hi, Coreg. Come on in."

"Hello, Lettie. You look amazing in that dress. Did Andrea make it?" the Levassian asked.

"She did. Isn't is gorgeous. I can't wait to show it off at the communal meal," she said.

"Hello, Andrea, PJ. Andrea, you look wonderful in that pink. You've done something to what you're wearing. I like it," Coreg said.

"Thank you."

"We better go so that we get there ahead of the worst of the crowd. It will be easier to get our meal and find a table," Coreg said.

Andrea and Lettie were tucked between the two men as they walked toward the town's community center. There would be booths where many Levassians showed off their wares to peruse, as well as music and the chance to talk with some of the other women from the doomed ship. Andrea enjoyed it when they ate there.

The closer they got to the communal center, the more people joined them on the walk there. Several of the women commented on both her and Lettie's clothes. They immediately asked for something to be made for them when they found out that Andrea had made them. She was going to be very busy. The thought broadened her smile as they walked up to the covered center where dozens of people already gathered.

"Let's get in line to get our food," PJ said. "I'm starved. We were busy today."

"I heard that you've been able to repair several of the old irrigation systems. That is a great benefit to our crops," Coreg said.

"Several of us worked on mechanical machinery back on Earth. I'm glad we can do something useful here," he told the other man.

"Look, Lettie. Here comes Tegrig and Honrig. Their mouths are open." Andrea smiled at Lettie's sudden nervous fiddling with her dress. "Calm down, hon. They aren't going to bite."

"I can't help it. I'm not used to anyone staring at me like they do. I feel like I'm a bug under a microscope around them," she said.

"If you're not attracted to them, I can get PJ to ask them to leave you alone," Andrea told her.

"No. Don't do that. I like them. They just make me feel weird."

"That's attraction, hon. Go with it. If you get too weirded out, just signal me, and I'll help you out."

"Lettie. You look amazing. Where did you get that beautiful garment?" Honrig asked.

She looked over at Andrea before drawing in a deep breath. "Andrea made it for me. Isn't it lovely?"

"You are lovely in it," Tegrig said.

"Would you honor us by sitting with us?" Honrig asked.

Lettie looked over at Andrea as she reached out to take the plate being offered to her. PJ rescued the other woman by answering for her.

"If you sit at a table next to ours, she can sit with you. She's not used to you yet, so I don't want her too far in case she becomes nervous," PJ said.

"Of course. We understand," Honrig said.

"Allow me to carry your plate," Tegrig told Lettie as he took it from her hands.

Andrea watched as Lettie smiled shyly up into the other man's face then let them lead her toward a table near the center of the covered area.

"She's a little overwhelmed by their attention," Andrea said.

"They are smitten with her," Coreg told her. "They will treat her well."

"Just the same, we'll sit next to them," PJ said.

"It is good that you are protective of her. It proves that you are an honorable male who would watch after a female not part of your family unit," Coreg said.

"She's like a sister to me," Andrea told him.

"I'm sure she feels the same way. She looks up to you." Coreg took her plate along with his and led them toward a table next to the one Lettie and her men were sitting.

When she sat down, PJ sat on one side of her and Coreg the other. She felt cocooned between them. The feeling wasn't unpleasant. She liked being between them where she felt safe and cared for. Andrea looked over to where Lettie was blushing and giggling between the two Levassian men. She hoped that the three of them could work things out. Lettie needed a home where she felt safe and loved. She was so young to have been sent out, but then many of the women sent out into space had been under twenty-two or twenty-three.

Andrea listened as Coreg and PJ talked about the planet's agriculture system and the talks of needing to expand the fields to accommodate the humans and the promise of future children. She could hear the excitement in Coreg's voice as he relayed some of the things being bounced around by the council.

"There are older cities on the other side of the fields that were abandoned when we began to die out. It's possible that we will begin to send males over to build a wall around them like the one here and refurbish them for future generations," Coreg said.

"Isn't that planning a little far ahead? It will be years before any children born in the next five or so years are old enough to need any place to stay. From what I've heard, there are still plenty of empty homes here in Levastah. You have been losing a few of your men every year now. That will increase over the years."

"You're right. Still, they are excited and thinking ahead. It is good that our people have something good to look forward to again. It has been a long time since we've held hope in our hearts," Coreg said.

Andrea smiled, happy that the two men were getting along so well. The more time she spent around Coreg, the more she liked him. He wasn't rude or demanding of her or PJ, and he was sweet to Lettie.

"Everyone is looking at Lettie's dress, Andrea," PJ said, sounding proud as if he'd created it himself.

"She looks amazing in it," Andrea agreed.

"You will have everyone on your doorstep wanting one for themselves now," Coreg told her.

"I don't mind. It will be fun sewing again." She stopped and looked up at the Levassian male. "Will the men in the shops who made our dresses get angry with me for taking away their business?"

"No. They will be curious as to why they like your dresses over theirs, but they won't mind. They have plenty to keep them busy with all of our needs. Do not worry yourself over such. Your happiness is all that matters." Coreg smiled down at her.

They finished up their meal then visited with others at the pavilion before returning home. She'd agreed to see several other women the next day about fitting them for dresses. She couldn't wait to get started.

Coreg stopped at the door to their home and said goodnight to Lettie and PJ, then smiled down at her and lowered his head to place a chaste kiss on her lips.

"If you don't mind, I'd like to visit you again the day after tomorrow. I will be working late tomorrow and unable to visit."

"The day after tomorrow is fine, Coreg. I'll look forward to it. Why don't you plan to eat with us?"

Coreg's face lit up like a third sun. Why would he get so excited that she'd asked him to supper? It puzzled her, but she didn't worry about it. She was just pleased that he wanted to come.

"I will see you soon, Andrea. Be safe and happy." Coreg turned and walked off toward his home.

Chapter Four

PJ pulled Andrea into a warm embrace as he got ready to leave for work. She wrapped her arms around his waist and smiled up at him.

"Wish you didn't have to work all the time," she said.

"I don't really work all that much. Got to feel productive and it's only fair since we're living in their homes and eating their food," PJ reminded her.

"I know. I miss you though."

"I like that you miss me. I miss you, too. I'll be home before supper time. Don't forget you invited Coreg to eat with us. That's some kind of big deal according to the Levassians from work. Means you're accepting him." PJ kissed her lightly on the lips then a little deeper. "Maybe we should sit outside tonight for a while. Without Lettie around."

"What do you mean?" Andrea asked.

"I think you and Coreg need to decide if you're compatible or not before this goes any further. I like the man well enough, but you're the one who needs to be sure."

"Oh. I suppose you're right. I was taking it slow, but I guess that isn't working very well if I've already indicated that I'm accepting him. I hate not knowing all the rules here," she said.

"Yeah. It's like moving to a foreign country like France or Germany and not knowing the customs. You can get yourself into trouble fast if you make the wrong move."

"I do like him, PJ. Are you okay with this? I mean really?" she asked.

"Yeah. We all agreed when we got here that we'd continue to live in threes and accept a Levassian as one of the males in the family. I'm glad you picked Coreg. I like him better than some of the men here. Some are too formal and condescending to me."

Andrea chuckled. "I know what you mean. The male at the clothing shop Coreg took me to the first time I met him was like that."

"We'll make this work, Andrea, if it is what you want. As long as he doesn't hurt you, I'm fine with him being a part of our family."

"Thanks, PJ."

Andrea stood up on her toes and pulled PJ down for a kiss. A real kiss. She opened to him as he thrust his tongue inside her mouth. He explored her as if he'd never tasted anything as sweet as her before. When he slowly pulled back, Andrea was out of breath.

"I'll see you tonight, babe."

"Be safe, PJ."

Andrea watched him walk away to disappear round the corner. She did miss him when he was gone. They'd grown close over the months since they'd crashed on the strange planet with its two suns and the blue moss-like grass that covered the ground where there were trees, or under the shadows of the houses. It was all so strange, yet she felt as if she'd lived there for years instead of months.

"Hey, Andrea. Is now a good time to come for a fitting?" One of the women from the night before walked up carrying a large amount of light blue material.

"Hey. Yes. Now is perfect. Come on in out of the suns." Andrea led the way inside to the living area where her sewing station was set up.

For the next four hours she worked with two of the women she'd agreed to sew for, then ate a light lunch with Lettie. The other woman suggested that they both needed a nap after eating. She eyed her machine but agreed that she was a little tired and could use the downtime. She followed Lettie down the hall to where their sleeping rooms were and said good-bye to the other woman, then slipped into her room.

She didn't immediately fall asleep but found herself drifting, thinking about Coreg and PJ and if she was truly serious about the Levassian. Something had drawn her to him almost from the instant she'd met him back on that street days earlier. She couldn't help but be interested in him when he'd shown her nothing but gentleness and a sense of awe in the way he looked at her.

Andrea felt as if she was the only person in the world to him when he looked at her with his bright silver eyes. Even the light, easy kisses he'd given her aroused her. Her pussy grew damp even now just thinking about him and those sweet kisses. What would it be like if he truly kissed her as a man kissed a woman? Like how PJ had kissed her that morning.

I'm sexually attracted to him. I like him, and he treats me like a princess. What more do I need to know about him?

She wanted him as a woman wanted a man and it felt the same as the way she wanted PJ. The only difference was that she wasn't at all sure how it all worked with Levassians. So far there were two women who'd taken in one or two of the men from the planet, and they were obviously extremely happy and expecting babies. That meant something worked. It was that little seed of worry that held her back from saying hell yes to taking on Coreg. What could she expect when it came to sex? They were big men. Much larger than human men. Would it hurt to have sex with one of them?

Andrea finally drifted off to sleep into a dream where she and Coreg and PJ had wild monkey sex that was nothing like what she imagined it would be like in real life.

* * * *

"He's here," PJ announced from the living area just before a knock sounded at the door.

"How did you know?" Lettie asked with a laugh.

"Heard him on the porch. He's kind of heavy-footed," PJ said.

"He would be. He's a big man," Andrea said from the living area. "Let him in."

PJ opened the door and invited him inside. He shook PJ's hand then smiled at Lettie, and finally over at Andrea where she sat behind her sewing machine putting together yet another dress.

"Hello, Coreg. How was work today?" she asked.

"It was a productive day. We're in the middle of harvesting before the cooler weather hits."

"Your idea of cooler weather is nothing like our idea of it," PJ said with a laugh. "It doesn't get cold here like it did on Earth."

"I have heard of this cold wet white stuff that falls on your planet in your winter time. It sounds pretty but nasty at the same time," Coreg said.

"Even though it doesn't get that cold here, I'm looking forward to the cooler weather where I can sit outside without sweating like a pig," Andrea said.

"Pig. That is an animal on Earth?" Coreg asked.

"Yes, but pigs don't really sweat," PJ said. "It's just a saying we have."

"I see."

Andrea could tell that he really didn't. "Come on in. Last meal will be ready in a little bit. Lettie is finishing up." Andrea pushed aside the dress she'd been working on and held up a small outfit she'd made from the left-over material of the dresses. "What do you think about this for the babies? I thought to make a few of them for each of the babies for when they're born."

Coreg gently touched the garments and smiled. "Those are perfect for the young. I'm sure the families will be honored to have such. That is very kind of you to create such things for them."

"They are going to need clothes, so I'm going to start drawing up some patterns for children's clothes to make for them. I'm sure your clothiers will have trouble with those large machines they have creating small garments for the children," Andrea pointed out.

"You are probably right about that. It has been many years since there's been a need for anything that small." Coreg touched the garment again. "I'm impressed by your talent, Andrea."

"She's amazing when it comes to sewing. That's for sure." PJ pulled her into a sideways hug then let go.

"Hey, Coreg. It's great you could eat with us. The meal's ready if you guys are." Lettie walked into the room wiping her hands on a cloth.

"We're ready." PJ ushered Andrea ahead of him with Coreg behind him.

They fixed their plates then sat around the table eating and chatting. Coreg told them about harvest and what all they did during that time. PJ asked questions and made comments about how it was done on Earth.

Andrea and Lettie exchanged eye rolls on occasion at the way the men talked and boasted about their work. She enjoyed herself and liked that the two men could talk so easily.

Once the meal was finished, she and Lettie cleaned up then joined the two men in the living area where they had continued their chat about work. Andrea sat between the two men as if she'd always been sitting there. Lettie sat on a chair and joined in, talking about Tegrig and Honrig. She'd talked with them on the communication unit each evening after the meal.

When the communication unit sounded a little later, Lettie's face turned a pale red at the knowing looks PJ and Coreg gave her.

"Let's go outside and give Lettie some privacy," Andrea suggested with a wink in the other woman's direction.

"That's a good idea," PJ said.

She and the two men walked outside and settled on one of the long benches that lined the patio like porch out front. Once again, Andrea found herself between the two men. It wasn't an uncomfortable place to be, but she couldn't help but feel a bit nervous.

"Andrea, I am not sure if you knew the importance of asking me to eat last meal with you tonight, and feel it is only fair that I explain it to you in case you didn't mean it in that manner," Coreg began.

"What do you mean?" she asked.

"When a female asks a male to share last meal, it means she is interested in joining with him, sexually. It is also how she introduces her family to a male she is interested in forming a family unit with." Coreg looked out into the darkening street.

"I see. You're thinking that I might not feel that way despite the fact that I asked you to eat with us." Andrea watched the man's face.

She could see in the way his eyes squinted though there was no sun in his eyes that it was what he worried about.

"I wanted to be sure you were aware of the custom of our people. I should have told you before accepting the invitation, but I was desperate to see you again," he said finally, turning to look down at her.

"I am interested in you, Coreg. PJ and I've talked and he understands that I am attracted to you as a woman is to a man or male. I think we could make a good family together, but I need a little more time to get to know you. Is that going to be a problem for you?" she asked.

His eyes widened and sparkled all at the same time. She could see relief flow over his features like water over a gentle brook. Coreg was obviously fine with that.

"I'm honored, little one. I understand you need more time. We have plenty of time. I will admit to being anxious as I'm very attracted to you, but your happiness and contentment are more important than how I feel. Please allow me to visit often so that you may become more accepting of me." Coreg's words tumbled over each other when he spoke.

Andrea couldn't help but chuckle. "You're welcome here anytime you want to come by. Um, PJ. You don't mind if he comes when you're not around do you?"

"No. He's welcome as a potential member of our family unit." PJ looked at Coreg. "Is that what I'm supposed to say to clear it that you're welcome to visit?"

Coreg bowed his head at PJ. "Thank you for learning our custom and making me feel welcomed, PJ. I won't overstep my welcome. I just want Andrea to become comfortable around me that she might agree to include me in your family unit."

"Don't worry, Coreg. Half the battle is already won. She likes you," PJ told him.

Coreg leaned over and cupped Andrea's cheek with his hand. "May I kiss you, little one."

"Please. I'd like that."

He leaned down and touched his lips to hers. She reached up and pulled him closer with one hand around the back of his neck. He deepened the kiss, pressing harder against her lips until she parted them, allowing his tongue access to her mouth. He licked and touched every part of it, then thrust his tongue in and out as if mimicking what he'd like to be doing to her.

When they separated, Andrea was panting. Her pussy had grown wet, dampening her panties. Coreg ran his nose down the side of her cheek to her neck where he inhaled then nipped at the tender flesh before pulling back.

"You smell ripe and delicious, Andrea. I could make a meal off of you. I'd better go before I can't control myself." He stood up.

Andrea reached out to grasp his hand. She squeezed it and gave him a warm smile. He returned it then was gone.

PJ squeezed her other hand. "I think you got him a little too close to attacking you, babe. You don't know your own strength."

Andrea's face grew warm. She could feel the heat all the way down her neck. Even her nipples felt hot and tender against the shift she wore.

"I might have gotten a little hot and bothered myself," she admitted.

"Think you feel comfortable enough to mess around a little? Watching you with Coreg got my dick hard. I'd love to taste that hot pussy of yours."

Andrea's face grew even warmer, if that were possible. "I'd like that. I'm pretty turned on."

"I can tell. Your nipples are poking through that dress you have on."

She instantly covered her breasts which had PJ chuckling. They were sitting outside and her tits were poking out. She stood and immediately walked toward the door.

"I hope Lettie's finished her conversation with Tegrig and Honrig," she muttered as she opened the door.

Fortunately, the woman was nowhere in sight. She'd probably returned to her sleeping room for the night. Andrea allowed PJ to pull her down the hall to his sleeping room next to hers. Lettie's was on the other side of Andrea's.

"You're sure about this, Andrea? I don't want to drag you into anything you aren't ready for." PJ opened his door with a palm to the side but hesitated.

She smiled and walked inside the room, tugging on his hand as she did.

Chapter Five

"You're so freaking hot, Andrea. I can't wait to taste your sweet pussy." PJ couldn't help himself. He wanted to feel her on his tongue and find out if she were spicy or super sweet like she smelled.

Andrea sighed against his chest as he held her tightly in his arms. She shivered as if cool, but he knew it was from excitement. He pulled back and looked down into her heavy-lidded eyes. She was beautiful in her arousal. PJ kissed her then ran his tongue down her jawline to her neck where he nibbled before retreating. He needed to undress her. He wanted to see her luscious body. She was curvy in all the right places like a woman should be.

"You go to my head like smooth whiskey, babe. I can't wait to see you naked."

PJ began lifting the material of her dress up her back until he had the bottom of it in his hands. He slowly pulled it over her head then tossed it to one side. He looked down to see that she wore nothing but panties beneath it. No wonder he'd been able to see her nipples through the lightweight garment. Her nipples were hard and thick with a wide dark ring around them. He bent down and sucked one of the hard nubs into his mouth and moaned.

Andrea's swift intake of breath told him she liked what he was doing. He switched nipples then let it pop from his mouth. PJ walked her backward until she hit the edge of his bed. Then he pressed down on her shoulders so that she sat on the mattress. He knelt between her legs and used one hand to press her down so that she lay against the mattress while he slowly pulled her panties over her hips and down her legs. Once he had them off, he leaned in and inhaled her sweet scent.

She smells better than coffee when I first get up in the morning. I can't wait to taste her.

He leaned in and spread her pussy lips, admiring how they glistened with her arousal. He slid his tongue up the slit and groaned at the tart taste of her juices.

"Better than coffee, babe. I could wake up to this every morning and be happy," he told her.

"You love your coffee," she said in a breathless hiss.

"I think I love the taste of you more."

PJ ran his tongue all around her little bundle of nerves until it stood out from the protective hood. Then he lapped at the slit once more. She lifted her hips with his licks as if not wanting the contact to end. He smiled as he enjoyed her unique taste.

When her breaths began to come in soft pants, PJ entered her tight sheath with one finger, pumping it as he licked around her clit. When she seemed to have adjusted to that one, he added a second finger and pumped them in and out until she was lifting along with his thrusts.

"Oh, God, PJ. I'm close. I'm so close."

He smiled and pumped faster, then sucked on her clit until he heard her scream his name. He brought her down with soft strokes of his tongue and one hand to her abdomen to hold her still. She gasped and panted for several seconds before she was able to say anything to him.

"That was, oh God. It was so good." She lifted her arms and tugged at her long black hair. "I'm worthless now."

PJ laughed. "I'm not finished with you yet, babe."

"Give me a second and I'll take care of you. Just need to catch my breath."

"I've got this, babe."

PJ crawled up the bed and knelt next to her head. He grasped his cock with one hand and played with her breast with the other. He wasn't going to fuck her without Coreg. It wasn't really fair. He'd jack off on her breasts and be fine with that for now. All he cared about was that he'd taken care of her first. He had no idea how Levassians took care of their women sexually, but humans, good ones, took care of their women first.

To his surprise, Andrea opened her mouth and wrapped her hand around his to pull his dick closer. She stuck out her tongue and licked across the bulbous head before licking at the slit. He nearly came on the spot.

"Damn, Andrea. Your tongue feels good."

"Let me have you for a second, PJ. I want to taste you like you tasted me."

He released his hold on his shaft and watched as she brought his cock down to her mouth where she sucked it in and ran her tongue around the width of him. She sucked down on him then slowly backed off until just the cockhead remained in her mouth.

"Holy, fuck, babe. That's so damn good." PJ couldn't look away from the sight of her mouth around his dick.

She hummed around him as she sucked him back down then swallowed around him.

"Fuck. Yeah. Just like that." He groaned, squeezing his eyes shut for a second at the amazing feel of her throat convulsing around his dick.

"That feels so fucking good. I'm going to come if you don't stop, babe. Let me finish on your tits this time. I want to see my cum on your body." PJ gently pulled from her mouth despite the suction of her mouth.

"You taste good, too, PJ. I love the saltiness in my mouth."

"You can suck me off another time if you want to. I promise, babe." PJ's voice wobbled.

He was so damn close to shooting his load. He squeezed the base to help him calm down. It didn't help much though because Andrea reached beneath his body to cup his balls in her hand.

"Damn, babe. You're not going to make this easy on me, are you?"

"I like touching you. I like seeing that out of control look on your face and knowing I put it there." Andrea's eyes lowered slightly as she watched him tug on his dick.

He pumped it up and down as she gently squeezed and tugged on his balls. He could feel the cum boiling in them. He wanted to drag it out some, but with her playing with him and that look of satisfaction on her face, PJ knew it wouldn't be long before he was spewing all over her chest.

"Yeah, babe. Squeeze them just like that. I'm gonna blow, babe." PJ's ass cheeks contracted, squeezing as his dick erupted, shooting cum all over Andrea's breasts and chest.

His head fell backward as his eyes nearly rolled back in his head from the pleasure he felt at coming. Not just coming, but coming with Andrea's hand on his balls. Fuck that was hot.

He ran his fingers through his jism and rubbed it into her breasts and chest before collapsing on the bed next to her.

"Give me a minute and I'll clean you up, babe. I'm done for right now."

Her giggle made him turn his head to look at her. She was looking at him with a broad smile on her face. He liked seeing it there. She'd enjoyed it as much as he had and that did it for him. She hadn't been grossed out with his need to mark her. He'd worried a little about it just before he'd come, but now he could see it had all been for nothing. She was perfect.

"I can always get up and shower off, PJ. You can relax, but don't fall asleep before you undress. You won't sleep well wearing your clothes."

"Don't go anywhere. I'll be right back."

PJ forced himself up and walked over to lay a hand on the wall where a sink popped out. He turned on the hot water and wet a cloth to clean her up. He walked back to the bed and climbed on. He gently cleaned her with the warm, wet cloth. Then he kissed her and backed off the bed to undress.

It didn't take him long. He climbed back on the bed and pulled Andrea into his arms.

"Sleep here with me, babe. I like having you in my arms."

"I like being in them.

* * * *

Andrea and Lettie chatted with Sandra, who'd come over to see about having a dress made. She'd brought several of her shifts that Andrea planned to use to make a more fitted garment for the woman. She brought news about what all was going on in Levastah. She and another woman from the ship lived with two cousins until they chose men for their family units. Sandra said she wasn't in any hurry. She'd met several of the Levassians who she liked, but hadn't made up her mind.

Her friend was planning to choose Corey Hallows from the ship and a Levassian she'd met while eating at the pavilion, but wasn't ready to make the commitment yet. The woman was a little unsure of the Levassian culture and wanted more time to get used to everything. Andrea understood that need. It was a lot like the way she felt. She wanted to feel completely comfortable around Coreg before they moved in together.

On top of that, she didn't know what they would do about Lettie. She couldn't stay by herself and she wasn't ready to commit to Tegrig and Honrig yet. She'd have to come with them when they moved into Coreg's home. She was sure that's what they'd do since family units lived in a family home, and the one they were living in wasn't Coreg's.

After Sandra left, Andrea got to work on one of the other garments she'd been working on while Lettie looked through the history of Levastah on the communications unit. She was enjoying learning about the Levassian people. She'd shared a lot of what she'd learned with Andrea. She was learning about them without having to read all the information. Lettie seemed to love reading.

Several hours later, there was a knock on the door. Andrea had just gotten up to get something to drink, so she waved Lettie back to her reading and answered the door herself. It was Coreg.

"Hello, Andrea. Would now be a good time to visit with you?" he asked.

"Yes. Come on in. Would you like something to drink? I was just about to get some of that flavored water you guys drink."

"Thank you, Andrea. That would be nice."

Coreg followed Andrea into the kitchen area and sat while she poured for them. He accepted the glass she handed him and smiled as he took a sip.

"You look wonderful today, little one. The color of your dress brings out the sparkle in your eyes."

Andrea felt heat pour into her cheeks. She always grew embarrassed when he complimented her. It wasn't something she was used to.

"Thank you."

"I was hoping that maybe you and PJ would have last meal at my home at the end of the week. I believe he's off that day. I would like to cook for you," he said.

"I'd like that. I'm sure PJ will be fine with it, but I'll ask him tonight." Andrea figured that this had to be a step in the direction of becoming a family unit in their culture.

"Do you think you'd get too hot if we sat in the back gardens? The cover will protect your sensitive skin."

"That's fine. I don't mind going outside. I haven't sat back there much at all."

She stood and followed him to the back door that led out to a covered patio where pots of flowers bloomed in stunning shades of silver and gold. There were even some bronze and yellow flowers amid the lush blue and tan colored foliage.

Andrea sat on one of the benches made of some type of material similar to concrete, but it was metallic looking. A cushion kept the surface from digging into her legs. Coreg sat next to her and wrapped one arm around the back of her shoulders, pulling her closer to him.

"I wanted some privacy that we could touch and talk. I hope that is all right with you," he said.

"It's fine. With Lettie around, it's hard to find a way to be alone."

"She's a sweet female. She is welcome to live with the three of us once you are comfortable enough to share my home."

Andrea smiled though she knew he couldn't see it. "You are sure that we will join, aren't you?"

Coreg stiffened and pulled back. "I'm sorry. Am I reading too much into how everything is progressing?"

"No. No. I'm sorry. I was teasing you. That wasn't very nice of me. I'm not used to how you guys see things. I'm comfortable with our joining eventually once I'm a little more used to being around you, Coreg. I didn't mean to imply that I wasn't."

His posture relaxed, and he pulled her close to him again. "I am overly sensitive because I want you so much. Please forgive me, little one."

"There's nothing to forgive. I was the one who caused the misunderstanding. I really like you, Coreg. I'm coming to care about you a great deal. I think spending time between the two of us is a great way for me to become used to being around you."

"I agree. The more I see you, the more I know you are right for me. No one is more beautiful in my eyes." Coreg kissed her forehead then leaned her into his embrace so that Andrea rested her head against his shoulder. "What are your views on having young, Andrea?"

She jerked then relaxed. It was a fair question. It was one that all couples needed to discuss before marriage. This was no different.

"When we were chosen to go to a new planet, one of the things that was important was that we were able to have children and we were expected to have them once we'd settled on the planet. I want children, Coreg. I don't know how many, but at least two. I guess it depends on how difficult it is to have them."

"I want young as well. I would love to have at least two if not four, but I wouldn't want you to go through a difficult birth if that happens for you. I will be honored just to have one," he said.

"I can't wait to see what Della and Caro's children look like when they are born. I think the entire city is waiting on them."

"You are right. I know the elders are busy planning celebrations for them. Will you attend them with me? PJ, too, of course."

"Absolutely. Also, I plan to deliver the children's clothes to them in a few weeks. I want to have at least six outfits each. I should be finished with them soon."

"I would be honored to escort you to see them if PJ isn't able to."

Andrea smiled up at him. "I'd like that."

Coreg lowered his head and turned her so that he was able to kiss her. His mouth plundered hers with an eagerness that spoke volumes to how much he wanted her. She could feel his arousal against her hip when he pulled her to sit on his lap.

"I can't lie to you, Andrea. I want you so badly that I hurt. I relieve myself each night thinking about you. Do you think of me at night, little one?" he asked.

"I do. My pussy gets wet wondering what it will be like to have sex with you."

"I will be very careful with you, Andrea. I would never willingly hurt you. I promise this."

"I know, Coreg. I can feel how large you are. It might take some adjusting, but we'll make it work."

"When the three of us join, I will not be able to come into your sweet ass. I am afraid that I will hurt you."

Andrea shivered at the thought of taking both men at one time. She knew all about anal sex. It was one of the things that had been taught on the spaceship. It was one of the ways a threesome bound to each other so that there was no jealousy between the two men. She'd nearly forgotten about it after the crash.

"Don't worry about it now, Coreg. We'll work everything out between the three of us when we get to that point."

"Just as long as you know that I will not hurt you and will make sure you are always protected."

"I know. I trust you just as much as I trust PJ."

"Will you let me love you now, Andrea?"

"What?" She nearly jerked out of his lap.

"I want to bring you to completion with my mouth. It would make me feel good, little one."

"Coreg, you don't have to do that."

"I know, but I want to. I want to taste you, have some part of you to get me through our courtship."

"Out here?" she asked.

"There is no one close by and we can put down the privacy shields," he said.

"There are privacy shields? I didn't know that."

Coreg moved her back to the bench then went to the side of the door and touched something there before moving to the edge of the patio to press on one of the columns that held up the roof. Strange screens lowered that allowed in the light and provided a slightly obscure view of the garden beyond.

"No one can see in and I've locked the door to the house so that Lettie won't accidentally walk out here while I have my mouth on your pussy."

Andrea's body heated at the idea of Coreg licking her down there. Part of her was thrilled at the naughty feeling of having oral sex outside, and part of her was just excited to do it with Coreg. She had no idea what to expect from the Levassian.

Chapter Six

When Andrea didn't protest, Coreg got to his knees in front of her and slowly lifted her dress in case she changed her mind. When he could see her panties, the garment that human women wore beneath their shifts, he helped her stand before lowering it down her legs and helping her step out of it.

He could smell her arousal. Good, she was getting excited at the thought of him licking her. Coreg wanted her excited and aroused. If he could bring her to completion with his mouth, he knew they would be compatible.

I will make sure she is always satisfied even if I must take care of myself at a later time. She always comes first.

He spread her legs wide to accommodate his broad shoulders then rubbed his nose in her womanly curls. The blackness of them contrasted with her pale pink flesh that surrounded her slit. He couldn't wait to taste her.

Andrea moaned when he nuzzled her inner thighs leaving light kisses along the tender flesh. He buried his nose at the juncture of her pelvis and hip, loving the musky scent of her there. He could lick her entire body and not grow tired of the contrasting tastes.

"I love the way you smell, little one. I can't wait to lick that pretty pussy. Relax for me. Let me love you."

He spread her pussy lips apart so that he could lick up her slit from bottom to top. He circled her tight bundle of nerves with his tongue then licked back down once again. Over and over he lapped at her juices like a man starved. She tasted like the Olevah plant, a mixture of sweet and tangy that was made into a drink that left

Levassians drunk when too much was consumed. Would he end up drunk on her? He wouldn't mind one bit.

She moaned when he stiffened his tongue and stabbed her slit with it. In and out, in and out. Coreg loved entering her like that. It reminded him that one day he'd be entering her with his stiff cock.

He lapped at her juices then entered her with one of his thick fingers. She groaned and lifted her hips toward him as he did.

"Easy, Andrea. I don't want to hurt you."

"More, Coreg. I need more," she whined.

Coreg pumped his finger in and out of her hot, wet cunt then added a second finger when he was sure she could accept it. She squirmed around him, her head thrashing back and forth.

"Oh, God, Coreg. I'm so close. Please don't stop."

"I won't, precious. Don't fight it. Come for me."

He continued pumping his finger in and out of her while he sucked on her tiny numb until she screamed around him. He couldn't stop the wide grin that spread across his face at knowing he'd done that for her. She'd come on his face with his fingers inside of her. Coreg felt like an honored warrior at having taken such good care of his female.

Andrea's whimpers grew weak as she slowly caught her breath while he cradled her on his lap. He'd redressed her, arranging her gown back into place after working her panties back on her body. He licked his lips, savoring every taste of her on his mouth.

"That was amazing, Coreg. Thank you. Won't you let me return the favor?" she asked.

"Thank you, little one, but not this time. I wanted to take care of you. I will be fine."

"It doesn't seem fair. I want to taste you as well."

"Another time. This time was for you and you alone. Thank you for allowing me to do it."

He cradled her in his arms and rocked her until he heard a soft snore. He looked down and smiled. She was asleep. He stood up and unlocked the door to carry her inside. He found Lettie talking with someone on the communications module and asked her which chamber was Andrea's

Lettie smiled. "The second one from this end."

Coreg carried her to her room and gently laid her on the bed, pulling an edge of the covers over her before kissing her lightly on the cheek and retreating. He said good-bye to Lettie and let himself out. It had been a good visit. He was proud of himself and confident that they would be a good match. He couldn't wait until they truly came together.

* * * *

Andrea fiddled with the material she was supposed to be creating a dress from. She kept looking toward the door in the entrance, waiting for PJ to walk in at any moment. Should she say something or pretend that nothing had happened between her and Coreg? She hadn't felt like this after she and PJ had messed around. Why did she feel as if she'd cheated with PJ?

I shouldn't feel this way. Is it because PJ and I were already friends from the ship?

She didn't know. All she did know was that her insides were churning like a storm on the ocean. She was afraid to work on the dress for fear she'd ruin it cutting off line. Instead, she was wrinkling it with her nervous hands.

The door opened and PJ walked in. He looked worn out. She smiled, hoping it looked natural.

"Hey. You look tired."

"Yeah. We worked on one of the machines they use for harvesting all day and still didn't get it going. I'm going to shower before we eat." He stomped out of the living area in the direction of his chamber.

Andrea breathed a sigh of relief that she had a little longer before she had to say anything. She figured that Lettie would say something over the meal about Coreg visiting if she didn't tell PJ first. That didn't need to happen. He might think she was keeping it from him.

Twenty minutes later, PJ returned with a more relaxed expression across his face and in the slant of his shoulders. He leaned down and kissed her before sitting next to her on the couch.

"Feel better?" she asked.

"Much. I hate it when we can't get something to work right. How was your day?" he asked. "Make lots of dresses?"

"I finished one and am about to start on another one. Coreg came by." Andrea looked down at her hands, avoiding PJ's stare.

"I figured he'd stop by since he was off today. Did you have a good visit?" he asked.

"Yeah."

PJ was silent a few long seconds. When he didn't say anything else, Andrea looked up and found him looking at her with a strange expression on his face. She quickly looked back down.

"And?" he asked.

"We talked."

"I have a feeling it was more than that or you wouldn't be acting this nervous." PJ pulled her closer with an arm around her shoulders. "Did something happen, babe?"

"I shouldn't feel this way," she finally blurted out.

"What way?" PJ asked.

"Like I cheated on you or something."

"What happened, Andrea?" he asked, his brows furrowing.

"We fooled around some."

"How?" PJ asked.

"Kind of like you and I did, only just with me."

PJ nodded, a ghost of a smile flitted across his face. Andrea couldn't tell if he was fine with it or if he was happy about it. Why would he be happy that she'd had oral sex with Coreg?

"So, he licked you until you came but you didn't reciprocate? Why are you all nervous over that if you're planning to accept him as our third?" PJ asked.

"I don't know. It just feels odd. You weren't here."

"Coreg wasn't here last night either. It's okay, Andrea. It's all part of getting used to the man and each other," PJ said.

"What if I'd, you know, given him oral sex back? Would you still feel the same way?" she asked.

PJ squirmed next to her. "No, I probably would have been jealous, but it would have been okay because we can't feel that way about each other. It's something he and I have to work out, not you. I don't want you to feel pulled between us. That's not how it should work."

"I don't want there to be hard feelings. I want us to be a family, and it does not matter if one of us has sex without the other one present. Maybe we need to go ahead and move in together so it doesn't feel like cheating as much." Andrea didn't know if that was the answer or not, but she hated the way she couldn't look PJ in the eye right then.

PJ seemed to pick up on her current mood when he squeezed her closer and kissed the top of her nose. He smiled at her when she finally managed to look up.

"It's okay, babe. I'm not upset with you at all. If you'd had sex I wouldn't have been angry with you. I'd have been disappointed that I wasn't a part of it, but it's your body that you're planning to share with two men, you shouldn't feel pressured about it. We'll work it out."

"I can't handle worrying about spending time with one of you over the other one. I'm serious about moving in together. Right now, I feel like I have to tiptoe around each of you as well as Lettie. If we move in together, maybe I won't feel so nervous about all of it," she said.

"That might be a good idea. Let's talk with Coreg about it and see what he thinks. I don't want to rush anything, but spending time with each of us alone is obviously worrying you."

"Was he coming over tonight for supper?" he asked.

"I don't know. I fell asleep and he put me to bed then left. Lettie said he didn't say anything before he left."

PJ smiled at her. "That good, huh?"

Andrea's face heated. "You're teasing me."

"Yep. You blush so nicely. I like seeing it on your face."

"Meanie. Why don't you call him and see if he wants to come over?"

PJ chuckled. "Good idea."

When he called up the communications unit, Andrea scooted to the far end of the couch. She didn't want to be in the viewing screen. Right then she felt all out of sorts and with her face all red she really didn't want Coreg to ask what was wrong.

"Hey, Coreg. Want to come over for last meal tonight? We can visit and talk." PJ asked when Coreg signed on.

"I would be honored to share last meal. I will come now if that would be okay."

"Perfect. Come on over. The meal should be ready soon." PJ signed off and shook his head at how Andrea was all squished up on the opposite end of the couch.

"You know he's going to see you when he comes over, babe."

"I know, but maybe my face won't be all red and splotchy when he gets here." Andrea jumped up and raced to her chambers to see what the damage was.

When she touched the wall to activate the mirror it was to find PJ behind her in the reflection. She whirled around and found herself in his arms.

"I don't like for you to worry so much, Andrea. Take a deep breath and calm down. There's nothing wrong with what you did or didn't do. Coreg and I will work out our feelings just like the three of us will work out being together."

"I know. I shouldn't feel conflicted, but with him living somewhere else and you being here it feels odd. I feel like I'm cheating when I spend time with either of you alone." Andrea drew in a deep breath and let it out slowly. "I'm trying to relax."

"Wash your face and take a minute. I'll let Coreg in and we'll sit down to eat. There's no need for all of this. I shouldn't have said anything about being jealous. Like I said, that's something Coreg and I have to work out between the two of us without involving you. Okay?"

She nodded. "Okay."

PJ pulled her into a tight hug then let her go and left her chambers, the door whooshing closed behind him. Andrea stared at the door long after he'd disappeared behind it. She was making more of this than was necessary. She needed to get a hold of herself.

She splashed cold water on her face then patted it dry. She added a bit of lip gloss to her mouth then stared at herself in the mirror. Her reflection told her that she'd failed to mask the unease in her eyes. She sighed. It would have to do. They'd talk after the meal and work things out one way or another.

The sound of someone knocking on the door when she exited her room had tiny moths flitting around in her stomach once again. Coreg was here.

Chapter Seven

Coreg stood after they finished the meal. "That was delicious, Lettie. You are a very good cook. Tegrig and Honrig should be proud of you."

"Thank you." Lettie blushed, her pretty face turning a cute shade of pink.

"Let's sit outside on the back patio and talk," PJ suggested.

Immediately, Andrea's face heated as well. Why did he have to pick the back? Did he know that was where they'd been when Coreg had brought her to climax with his mouth? Surely he wouldn't suggest it if he had known.

"That would be nice," Andrea said, flashing a quick smile in Coreg's direction.

To her surprise, he winked. It drove the burning sensation in her cheeks that much hotter.

Andrea followed the two men out to the covered back patio where Coreg activated the privacy screens once more. PJ nodded and sat in a chair at the round table while Coreg held another chair for her. She sat down, puzzled at PJ's choice of seating. Coreg took another chair and smiled at Andrea.

"How was your work today, PJ?"

"Frustrating. We're working on one of your older harvesting machines. They were better at harvesting some of the root vegetables than what you are currently using, but getting the thing to work is taking more effort than we anticipated," PJ told him.

"We are all very appreciative of your help with these old machines. We lost the knowledge of how to run them when our older males died. For many years, we had to harvest by hand then developed a few rudimentary machines that work faster, but not always better. Having the old ones back will be much more efficient and less work on our males." Coreg nodded at PJ.

"Did you enjoy your day of rest?" PJ asked the man.

"Yes. I visited some friends and stopped by and spent some time with Andrea." He smiled over at her. "I greatly enjoyed the time with her."

Once again, moths, a little larger this time, flitted around in her stomach.

"I enjoyed your visit as well. I'm sorry I conked out on you and you had to put me to bed. I guess I was tired from working on the baby clothes." Andrea knew her face showed her nervousness.

"I didn't mind at all, little one," Coreg said.

"That brings me to what we need to talk about," PJ began.

Coreg's face grew storm clouds. "Do not upset Andrea. I was the one who started it. I won't have her upset over this."

"I'm not angry and would never blame Andrea for something that was natural. It's the fact that she does feel nervous about spending time with either of us alone that I want to talk about it. I hate that she feels pulled between us." PJ reached over and covered her hand with his. "I merely want to discuss how we can make this easier on her."

"I apologize. I should have known that you wouldn't pressure her. I too, would like to make this as easy on Andrea as possible." Coreg relaxed back in his chair once more. "What do you suggest to make this smoother for all of us?"

"Actually, Andrea suggested a possible solution," PJ said. "She thinks we should go ahead and move in with you so that we are together more."

Coreg's face glowed at the suggestion. "I would welcome that, and I agree that it would help to spend more time together. There are four sleeping chambers in my pod, so there would be room for all of us, including Lettie."

"That's good, but I think we should plan to all sleep in the same room. We don't have to become intimate at first, but it would make the transition into a family unit as you call it, much easier," PJ suggested.

Andrea hadn't thought that far ahead, but it made sense. If they shared a room, a bed, they'd progress faster into feeling more comfortable around each other. She glanced over at Coreg then at PJ.

"I would be fine with that, PJ. Andrea? What about you? Would you feel comfortable sharing the main chamber with both PJ and I?" Coreg asked.

"Yes. I'm sure it will be a bit awkward at first, but I think PJ is right that it would help us grow closer if we share a room and a bed." Andrea smiled though she was still a little shaky concerning it.

"Coreg. I know that you and Andrea spent time together today and that you had oral sex. Andrea and I had oral sex the other night. I feel like we need to be completely honest with each other. I don't feel that we should tell each other every time we spend time alone with her after this, but I wanted it out in the open so that Andrea would begin to become used to the idea of alone time."

Coreg let out a long breath. "This is good. I didn't feel guilty, but I was worried about how Andrea would feel once I returned home. We should have talked about it afterward, but she fell asleep and I didn't want to wake her."

"So, we're on even ground now. Andrea, there's no need for you to worry about spending time with either of us in the future. It's all agreed that we're going to do everything possible to form a family and get used to each other."

"Okay. I'm sure I'm still going to feel a little antsy about it, but it will get better over time. When should we move in?" she asked.

"When are you next off, PJ? I will request that day as well and we can move you in together," Coreg suggested.

They continued talking long into the night, making plans and suggestions over how to work things out. Andrea was sure that most of what would need to be moved were her sewing machine and supplies. She smiled to herself. Instead of shoes and clothes, it would be what she enjoyed working on.

"How does that sound to you, Andrea?" PJ asked.

"Hmm? Oh, sorry. I was thinking about packing up my sewing things. What did you say?" she asked.

"How would two rotations from now work for you?" Coreg asked.

"That's fine. I can have everything packed away by then, and still finish the baby clothes I'm working on. I still want to carry them over to Caro and Della," she said.

"We'll do that once we're all moved in," PJ said. "I'm sure Coreg would like to go with us to do that."

"I would like us to go as a family unit," he said.

"Then it's settled." PJ stood up. "Let's call it a night. I'm beat and have a long day ahead of me tomorrow."

"I'll see myself out. Thank you both for agreeing to move into my pod. There will only be the two of us since I have no family sharing the space."

"You will have a new family now," Andrea told him, squeezing his hand as they walked back inside.

"I'm looking forward to many years with you, little one." Coreg kissed her then walked toward the front door. "I will see you in two rotations."

Once Coreg had left, PJ hugged Andrea close then led her to his chambers. She only hesitated a second before relaxing and joining him there.

"As much as I'd like to mess around with you, babe, I'm beat and really just want to hold you until we both fall asleep.

"That's fine. I'm a bit beat myself. Getting all emotional had probably drained you, babe. We can make up for lost time another night."

He pulled her into his arms and kissed her before letting her go and stripping off his clothes. Andrea did the same and slid into bed next to him. He pulled her into his arms, and within minutes, his steady breaths told her that he was asleep. Andrea smiled and snuggled next to him before falling asleep as well. Her last thought was to wonder how the three of them would manage to sleep once they were together.

* * * *

PJ and Coreg wouldn't let Andrea lift a finger as they carried their things inside Coreg's pod. The large dwelling contained three individual pods that each contained four sleeping chambers, a living room, and meal prep area. The front of the dwelling held a communal living space, and separate meal prep area for when they all wanted to share a meal. There were outside covered patios for each pod and the front held a communal porch that held several chairs and benches for the entire family to visit on cooler nights.

Coreg's was the far left pod. Andrea watched as they set her sewing machine and supplies on a table Coreg had brought in just for her machine. It sat to one side in the living room of their pod. She would have plenty of room to sew and piece together her dresses without worrying that she'd drop something as before.

"Thank you so much for finding the table for me, Coreg. I appreciate it. It will make sewing much easier for me," she told him.

"It was my pleasure to find something that would work for you. I know how much you enjoy sewing."

"Coreg, when you have a second, I need to know where to put our clothes," PJ called from the back of the pod.

Coreg smiled at Andrea then walked down the hallway to the main chamber.

Andrea quickly set up her machine then pulled out the dress she was working on and set it next to the machine. She arranged her supplies on one end of the table, then pulled out the twelve baby outfits she'd created, and wrapped each group of six in a swatch of cloth with ribbon to give to Della and Caro. She was super proud of the outfits, having never made anything that small before.

"Looks like you've just about got everything set up," PJ said.

"It's perfect. Is everything unloaded now?" she asked.

"Yeah. Come see the chambers and be sure we unpacked everything like you wanted."

"You already unpacked? I was going to do that." She jumped up and followed PJ down the hall to their new chamber.

Coreg showed her the closets. One was for her and the other one was for his and PJ's clothes. Both were spacious enough to hold many more outfits. Coreg showed her the drawers where her footwear and underwear was held. There were two empty ones if she needed them.

"What do you think?" PJ asked.

"It's great. There's more room than I thought."

"I'm pleased that you are happy with the chambers, little one." Coreg nodded his head toward her. "Let's take the young's clothes over to your friends' home."

Andrea couldn't help being excited to see if Della and Caro liked the outfits. She was also curious as to how the women looked now that they were pregnant. While Della might be having a normal human baby, Caro would definitely have one who was part Levassian and part human. Everyone was patiently waiting for them to give birth.

"Settle down, babe. You're rocking the transport," PJ said, smiling.

"No I'm not. Stop teasing me." She popped him on the shoulder.

"It is obvious that you are excited little one. How long has it been since you've seen the females?" Coreg asked.

"A couple of months. They don't go out anymore now that they're pregnant. I miss seeing them."

Coreg pulled the transport up to the home where both females lived. When PJ knocked on the door, Veran opened the door to them. He smiled and nodded to Coreg.

"It is good to see you, Coreg. This must be members of your family unit. Welcome to our home." Veran backed inside and opened the door farther. "We are pleased you have come to see us."

Sabin walked into the greeting hall and nodded. "It's good to see you, Coreg. Introduce us to the rest of your family unit."

"This is our female, Andrea. She's brought gifts for your females," Coreg began. "And this is PJ, our third."

"We are most pleased to meet you. Do come into the pod. Caro and Della are visiting in the communal living quarters," Sabin said.

As soon as they walked into the main room, Della and Caro squealed in excitement and jumped up the best their rounded bellies would allow. Immediately, the males rushed to help them up.

"Careful, female. You shouldn't get so excited and rush around," Veran said.

"Andrea. We haven't seen you in forever. You look great," Della said as she embraced Andrea.

Caro smiled and pressed her cheek to Andrea. "It's so nice of you to come visit. We don't see many people anymore. Our males keep us locked away so that nothing happens to us."

"That is not true, Caro. We are merely worried that you will overdo things. You tend to forget that you are carrying young," Sabin said.

"Don't worry. We can't forget that we have bowling balls inside of us," Della said, shaking her head.

"We've brought you gifts that our Andrea has made for your young," Coreg said.

"Sit down. The females need to sit with their feet up," Sabin said, urging Caro and Della back toward the couches where there were two beanbag looking things in front of it.

"I can't wait to see what you've made. Everyone is talking about your dresses," Della said.

"Right now, we're pretty comfortable in these drapes they made for us since we're sticking out in front, but as soon as we've lost our weight, Della and I both want dresses made," Caro said.

"I'd love to sew for you." Andrea handed each of the women their packages. "Since we don't know if you're having a boy or girl, they're generic in yellows and tans and oranges."

Della and Caro pulled the ribbon off and opened the material to exclaim at the jumpers she'd made for the babies. They held each one up for the men to see, then hugged each other with tears in their eyes.

"They're perfect, Andrea. We'd get up and hug you, but that's a tough thing right now. I doubt Sabin will let us," Della said.

"I'm so glad you like them. Once the babies are born, I can make some in pink or blue for you," Andrea told them. "They should fit for a few months at least."

"Levassian children are said to grow quickly. Plus, they are usually nine or ten of your human pounds. We know that Caro will have such a young, but we are not sure of Della's young right now," Sabin told her.

"I may not have one that large since I'm human," Caro told them. "In fact, you better hope I don't, or you may never touch me again."

Everyone laughed at her serious sounding threat. Andrea had a feeling that Caro wasn't joking. The idea of delivering a nine or ten-pound baby made her wince. That would definitely not feel good. Labor was hard enough without delivering a real bowling ball.

They visited for a few more minutes, then Andrea stood, seeing that the women were tiring and told everyone that it was time to return home.

"We've just moved in together and I need to see that everything is in the right place." She walked around to the couch and leaned over to hug each of the women. "I can't wait to welcome your babies into the world."

"Thank you so much for the baby clothes and for visiting. You must come back soon. We don't get many visitors," Caro said.

"I will. I've missed you guys." Andrea allowed PJ and Coreg to hold her hands.

"Oh, and congratulations on your joining," Della said. "It's great that you've found another male to make a home with."

Andrea knew she was blushing but couldn't stop it. It seemed she was doing a lot of that lately.

"It is a joyous occasion for the three of you. May your family unit prosper and flourish," Veran told them as he saw them out.

"Thank you, Veran. We are eager to meet the latest additions to your family unit. Wish Gressen and Kane good for us. We're sorry we missed them," Coreg said.

"They will be disappointed to have missed you, as well. They are gathering supplies before the last meal. Have a good trip back to your pod," Sabin said.

Andrea allowed PJ and Coreg to help her back into the transport. She'd had a great visit, though it had been short. She could tell that both Della and Caro were easily tired out. They only had about two months left before they delivered. Sooner according to what she'd learned about Levassians having their babies at eight months instead of nine. She wondered which of Della's men had fathered her baby. It would be odd if Caro had hers first, then a month later Della had a human child.

From what she'd been told by Coreg, the entire city of Levastah was eager for children of any kind. They didn't care if they were human or Levassian, or a combination of both. Andrea couldn't help but feel relief over that since she had a fifty percent chance of having a completely human child since PJ was one of her men.

Nine or ten pounds? It made her shutter.

"What's that look on your face?" PJ asked with a frown.

"Just thinking about going through childbirth knowing you might have a nine or ten-pound baby. That smarts," she said, shivering again.

PJ and Coreg chuckled. Andrea glared at them.

"You can't say anything. It's not your body that has to carry around a bowling ball then manage to force it out. If I get pregnant and go through that, I might shoot both of you."

Coreg winced. "I will pray that you have an easy time of your waiting. I would not want you to have pain, little one."

"You don't want me to kick you out of bed is what you mean," she said, glowering.

Coreg's face went almost white despite his silver skin tone. "You would make me leave?"

PJ laughed. "Don't worry, Coreg. She'll kick us both out for a few days then welcome us back once the pain is gone. Women tend to get very emotional when they're pregnant. You'll see."

"You have been around women during their waiting period?" Coreg asked.

"Yeah. My sister had twins before our planet began to go south. Talk about crazy. My brother-in-law never knew when he was going to be hugged and kissed, or have things thrown at him when he returned from working each day," PJ told him.

Coreg winced. "I wouldn't want to upset her and have things thrown at me."

"That's just it. You don't even have to do anything. Pregnant women's hormones go haywire and they go off over nothing." PJ squeezed Andrea's hand when she tried to pull it free. "He needs to know how women get during their pregnancy, babe. It's only fair."

"We aren't all crazy when that happens," she said.

"You've never been pregnant before. Don't make promises you can't keep, babe." PJ leaned over and kissed her.

"I will be very careful around you when you become with young, little one. I don't wish to upset you." Coreg took one hand and kissed the back of it.

Andrea sighed and shook her head. Once they started having sex, it was a very real possibility she'd end up pregnant sooner rather than later. Coreg hadn't had sex in forever or maybe even never at all. That hit her hard. The poor man had been celibate all his life as far as she knew. That was difficult to imagine when people from Earth had sex fairly often, even when they weren't married. What would it be like to have sex with a virgin?

Chapter Eight

"We're just going to sleep together tonight, babe. There's no need to be this nervous," PJ told her.

"I know, but it feels weird. I don't know why, except that there will be three of us in one bed."

"There would have been three of us if we'd made it to the other planet, Andrea. You were always going to have two men in bed with you at one time."

Coreg was in the cleaning unit. Andrea had already finished, and PJ was going to use it after Coreg was finished. It had finally sunk in that she was going to be sleeping with two men. One of which was an alien whom she'd only met a few weeks ago.

"I know. I know. I can't help feeling a little nervous. This is all new to me regardless of what was going to happen anyway. It's still different."

"Is it because I am not human, little one?" Coreg stepped out of the cleansing unit with a towel wrapped around his lower body.

"Damn." She sighed and plopped down on the bed wearing an overly large T-shirt. "Yes and no. I don't know. I think I'm just nervous of sleeping with a man period."

"I do not want you to be upset, Andrea. I can sleep in one of the other rooms if you prefer. There is plenty of time to try sleeping together. It doesn't have to happen right now if you are not ready," Coreg said.

"But I want us to be together. I'm just antsy." Andrea wrung her hands.

"Antsy? I'm not familiar with that word." Coreg looked at PJ.

"It means that she's nervous and can't be still," PJ supplied.

"Ah, I see," Coreg said.

"Why don't you get into bed, Andrea and we'll get in on either side of you once I get out of the shower? Will that work?" PJ asked.

"Um, yeah. Okay." Andrea stood and walked around to the side of the bed and climbed up. She sank into the mattress and pulled the covers up to her neck.

PJ chuckled. "I'll be right back, babe."

Coreg walked over to the bed and sat on the edge. "I do not like you to be so upset, little one. Are you sure you wouldn't rather us sleep in different chambers for a while?"

"I'm sure. I just need to relax. I've let this eat at me all day and shouldn't have."

"Andrea, just lie back and do not think about it for now. PJ will be out soon. Try to go on to sleep, little one."

Andrea sighed and tried to relax. She closed her eyes but didn't feel the slightest bit sleepy now. Why couldn't she get past this?

I want both of them, so why am I being so weird about this? I should be excited to finally have them both with me.

Coreg shifted on the bed next to her. Her eyes flew open at the movement only to see that Coreg had just moved an inch and hadn't laid down next to her. She sighed and turned to look at him.

"Are you really okay with sharing me with PJ, Coreg?"

"I am. It's more than I could have asked for, little one." He turned a little more to face her. "Think about it. Before you crashed on our world, we faced extinction and no future to speak of. Now, I have the chance to make a family with a female I adore. It only gets better that I like the other male in our relationship."

"I'm just worried that you and PJ will start to resent each other. I don't want that. I don't want to worry that somewhere down the line one of you will get dissatisfied and feel jealous or something."

"There's no guarantee that won't happen, but I don't foresee it. Here, there is no dissolving a family unit, or at least there wasn't before the scourge. I understand that on your Earth, you had divorce which did this. On our world, we work things out and avoid such situations. It will be the same with us, Andrea. You will see."

"I hope you're right. It would kill something inside of me if something came between us," Andrea said.

"If PJ and I have any issues, we will solve them between us. You will never feel that you have to deal with our problems. That is not the way of Levassians. A female is never pulled into a male's disagreements."

"There won't be about us."

"I want us all to be happy with this."

"We will be. Trust me, little one."

* * * *

PJ walked out of the cleansing chamber to find Andrea talking with Coreg. She looked worried or maybe anxious was a better word.

I don't like seeing her so worried and nervous. Did we push her too much by expecting us to sleep together the first night we're at Coreg's home?

He hoped not. He wanted them to be a family and part of that was sleeping together. By sleeping in separate rooms, they'd only be putting off the inevitable.

PJ liked Coreg. He was a good man and seemed totally devoted to Andrea. He couldn't ask for a better partner. The fact that they'd hit it off so quickly was even better than the planned relationship they'd had with Landon. She and Landon hadn't clicked like she had with Coreg. He couldn't ask for a better situation.

Now all he had to do was alleviate whatever fears Andrea still had about their relationship. He was completely on board with the threesome, or family unit as Coreg called it. All they needed to do was move toward the sex and everything would work out. He knew that making love would seal them closer than any marriage vows ever would.

Coreg stood up when PJ walked in. "We were just talking."

"Don't get up. We're going to bed anyway. It's late and I think we all need some rest," PJ said.

Andrea made sure she was directly in the middle and lay there as if moving would call out some monster to eat her. PJ hated seeing her so stiff and uncomfortable looking. He sighed then sit on the edge of the bed before stretching out.

"Andrea, relax. You're wound tighter than a pocket watch. Nothing is going to happen. We're just going to sleep. You'll never fall asleep that way."

"I've never slept in the same bed with two men before. I don't know what to do. I'm afraid if I move I'll touch one of you."

"There's nothing wrong with touching one of us. In fact," PJ said. "We're going to turn on our sides and scoot in close so that we're comfortable. You know, spoon together."

"What is spooning?" Coreg asked.

"Turn on your sides facing me."

Andrea and Coreg turned over so that Andrea was facing him and Coreg was facing Andrea's back.

"Now scoot closer. Andrea, you know what spooning is. Give me your arm over my side. Coreg, you scoot up behind Andrea and wrap your arm over her waist. Relax, both of you and we'll all get some sleep."

He could feel Andrea's stiff body behind him. As time went by, she slowly relaxed, and after about twenty minutes he could tell she'd finally fallen asleep.

"She's asleep now, Coreg. You can relax as well and get some rest."

"I don't like that our Andrea is so worried about this. Isn't there anything we can do to make this easier for her? Is she upset over having two men in a relationship?" Coreg whispered.

"No. She's just nervous about it. She knew she'd have two men in her life since we left Earth. That's not it. I think it is that she's not sure that you and I can agree over sharing her. I've tried to assure her that we're good with this, but it hasn't helped."

"I have also told her this."

"It will take time and experience."

"Experience?" Coreg asked.

"Seeing for herself that we won't fight over her."

"That is not how it is among my kind. We don't fight over things. We calmly talk them out and if we can't settle it, we go to the council and accept their decision."

PJ smiled to himself. "I don't think we will need to go that far. We just have to agree that any dispute between us never involves Andrea. She shouldn't have to know that we are fighting over anything, even if it doesn't involve her."

"I agree. That is best." Coreg shifted behind Andrea. "This spooning is nice. I like it, but having her ass near my cock is not helping me relax to go to sleep."

PJ chuckled. "Believe me. I'm in the same boat. My dick's so hard I could use it as a hammer."

"You use your male part as a hammer? Doesn't that hurt?" Coreg asked.

"It's just a metaphor. I wouldn't really do that, but that's how hard my cock feels." PJ couldn't stop the smile that spread over his face.

Living with Coreg would be amusing at times and comfortable at others. He truly hoped they didn't argue over anything, much less Andrea. He thought they would see eye to eye on most things. It was why he thought Coreg was a good match for him and Andrea.

"Are you good with the three of us, PJ? I know that Andrea surprised you when she wanted to introduce us. I pushed into her life by agreeing to go for her sewing machine."

"As long as Andrea is happy and you don't hurt her, I'm fine. Remember, we were already going to be in a threesome before we crashed, and since then, the council has stated that all family units would contain two men whether they are Levassians or humans. I'm impressed they didn't insist that at least one of you had to be in every relationship."

"They are happy as long as there are young in our lives once more. We've missed females, but also we've missed having young growing up here. We are all excited about the coming births from Caro and Della," Coreg said.

"I can tell. Everyone has been talking about it at work every day. They are really excited about it. They tell me that there have been all sorts of celebrations planned for them. Some have even created things for them like baby beds and highchairs."

Coreg's soft laugh behind Andrea barely reached PJ's ears. "Yes, I've heard that both women have more than they need for the upcoming births. I'm very proud of our Andrea for creating the tiny baby clothes. Our males have not been able to sew anything quite that small as of yet. They are working at it though, as there will need to be many outfits and even Andrea will not be able to keep up."

"She's so happy with her sewing. I appreciate that you took that chance and got it for her. It was dangerous for you, I know," PJ said.

"I had a soldier with my group. We were fine. I think we need to make more trips to the crashed ship and extract everything we can from it. I plan to discuss this with the council soon. There are many things the females would like to have that are not available here."

"Like what? What have you heard that they miss?"

"Those odd contractions that they wear beneath their clothes for one."

PJ laughed. "Bras. I for one would like that you don't find those."

"Why not?"

"Because they hide their breasts and limit the access we have to them."

"Ah, I see."

"That's me being a man, but they do provide some support for them. If you find them, I'd bring them back." PJ sighed. "What else have they asked for? I haven't heard anything."

"More of their clothes, personal items they were taking with them to the new planet. I don't know the details, only that they've asked for them."

PJ thought about it. "I think that's a good idea. It would go a long way to making them feel more at home here if they had some of their personal items to remind them of their past. You know, loved ones they left behind. I'm sure Andrea associates good memories with her sewing machine and being able to make things."

"That is what I thought. I will approach the council members tomorrow concerning this. I can truthfully tell them that it has made a difference in Andrea's happiness. They will attach a great amount of importance to making the females happy."

"You're a good man, um, male, Coreg. I'm ashamed to say that human men don't often put a lot of importance to making a woman happy. They just want them to be satisfied so that there's no drama in their lives and they still get sex."

"That is a dishonorable way to live. I am not surprised that your kind had this divorce I've heard of. If both parties in a relationship seek only to make the other one happy, there's no need for it."

"You're right, Coreg. You're right."

Chapter Nine

"You're doing what?" Andrea dropped the dress she'd been working on and stood up. "Why you?"

"Because I wish to help, little one. Finding that sewing machine made you happy. I want to help make all of you happy and it was my idea," Coreg said.

"It's dangerous. I should never have put you in that position. I'm ashamed of it now."

"Don't, Andrea. I was very happy to provide you with something that made you so happy. The males going with me are just as excited that they can bring this to all the females here. We should have organized it sooner, but thought you would be happy without all of it."

"I am, we are, Coreg. I'm scared something might happen to you. Let the others go. You've already been."

Coreg cupped Andrea's cheek with one hand. "I know most about where all the personal items stored in the holds of the ship are, so they don't waste time on other items. Those we can obtain another day. Once I show them the differences, I won't need to return and can leave it to the others."

"Please, Coreg. Don't go. I'm going to be so worried about you."

"Little one. I will be fine. There are several soldiers going with us plus eight other strong males. We will be fine. I will come here as soon as we are back and leave the unloading to them. I promise."

"Oh, Coreg. The fact that you want to help makes me proud, but I'm still worried about you going."

"I will back before dark. We will leave at dawn so that we have plenty of time to get there, load up, and return."

"Does PJ know about this?" she asked.

"Yes, he knows and will be staying home with you while I'm gone. He is of the same mind that it is needed in order to give the other females here a sense of comfort. We've talked about this already."

"See. That is what I've been afraid of. The two of you ganging up on me," Andrea said, snapping her hands on her hips.

Coreg's eyebrows shot up and his mouth widened into an O. "No, Andrea. We would never as you say, gang up on you. I truly didn't realize you would be so upset over this. That is why PJ is going to stay home with you, so you won't feel alone while I am gone. Plus, Lettie will be here."

"She spends some of her time with Tegrig and Honrig now. I'm glad you at least thought to have PJ stay with me. Otherwise I would have made myself sick worrying. I'm still going to be nervous until you get home."

Andrea realized that she felt like Coreg's house felt that way now. They'd developed a family unit and were getting used to each other being around all the time. Still, they hadn't had sex and that bothered her. She wanted to take it to the next step, but wasn't sure if she was ready for it. Once they had sex, made love, everything would be set in concrete. Deep down she knew that was crazy to think that way, but there it was.

"You promise you will be careful and not take any risks?" she asked, placing her hands on his chest.

"I promise, little one. I would never do anything that would take me away from you. You make my life joyous. You are the most important person to me."

"I guess there's nothing I can say to dissuade you, so I'll just keep quiet."

"You are my life, Andrea. I will not cause you pain."

Andrea stood on tiptoes and pulled Coreg's head down to kiss him. He deepened the kiss, placing one hand at the small of her back and the other one on her ass. She smiled into the kiss, thinking how male of him to grab her ass.

"What is so humorous to you?" Coreg asked pulling back.

"The fact that you grabbed my ass. It's something a human male would do."

"I've been taking notes from PJ on how to treat you. He often grabs your hind area."

"Evidently you are a quick study," she said, her mouth widening even more.

"We are okay now?" Coreg asked, his brows furrowing together.

Andrea sighed. "Yes. But if something happens to you I'll never let you forget it."

"I understand.

"Hey, you guys, what's going on?" PJ walked into the living area, home from work.

"Coreg just laid a bomb on me," Andrea said.

"What?" PJ frowned.

"About him going on another trip to the ship to get more stuff. I don't like it that you guys discussed it without me. I should have been in on it." Andrea pulled back from Coreg and fisted her hands at her hips once more.

PJ actually winced. "Sorry. I knew you'd be upset and wanted to put it off until today. Coreg insisted that he needed to be the one to tell you. I thought we should tell you together, but he was sure you'd understand better getting it from him."

"It's not fair for you two to gang up on me. It's two against one and I'll never win that way." Andrea crossed her arms and tapped one foot. "I won't stand for it, PJ."

"It won't happen again. I told you that if Coreg and I had a difference of opinions we'd settle it between us and not involve you, but you're right, if it concerns you outside of that, we should include you." PJ squeezed her upper arms then kissed her lightly on the lips. "It won't happen again, babe."

"You're darn right it won't. You'll both be in the doghouse if you try it again." Andrea glared at both men then returned to her sewing.

"What is this doghouse that she will put us in?" Coreg asked. "What is a dog?"

"You know those little Viggy things some of you have as pets? It's kind of like that. If you do anything that upsets your female, she will be angry and not talk to you or anything for a while. That means you're in the viggy house."

"Oh. That is not good then. Viggies don't like to share their sleeping space."

"Right. Do they have fleas?" PJ asked.

"What are fleas? I don't know that word either."

"Little biting insects."

"I don't believe so." Coreg eyed Andrea as if he was afraid of her wrath.

Well, he should be. I can't believe they talked about something this serious without me. Probably because they knew I'd never agree to letting Coreg go. If he hadn't already committed to it, I'd forbid him now.

Andrea knew it would make him look weak if she demanded he stay home now that it was all planned. She wouldn't do that to him. Still, it wouldn't stop her from sticking her nose up at him until time for him to leave in the morning. Then she'd hug and kiss him good-bye. She wasn't about to send him off worried about her feelings. He needed to be at top speed and watching out for himself instead of worrying about her.

She watched as the two men talked, smiling to herself as PJ attempted to explain doghouse to Coreg. They were so funny sometimes. It hit her then. She loved them. Both of them. They were important to her and did their best to make her happy and she loved them with all her heart. She wasn't sure when it had happened, but it had.

The two men walked outside as they discussed the trip Coreg was taking the next morning. She heard enough to know that PJ was giving him more directions to where things were in the hold of the ship. She was surprised and relieved that PJ hadn't wanted to go as well. That would have been more than she could have handled. More than likely PJ knew that and refrained from insisting.

How was she supposed to tell them that she loved them? Somehow just coming out with it didn't seem right, and telling them once they finally made love would cheapen it to her. Often words of love and devotion where spoken after sex that really weren't true. No, she wanted it to mean something when she told them.

Maybe she'd come up with a way while Coreg was gone on his mission. It would give her something to think about other than if he were okay out in the jungle with all the dangerous animals that Levasso had out there. Plus, she had her sewing to keep her busy. She smiled. She loved them and was sure that they cared deeply about her. Maybe that meant they would come to love her as well. She liked that idea, a lot.

Andrea thought about Della and Caro. They seemed to love their men a lot and the men doted on the women as if they were the most precious thing in their lives. She wanted that kind of relationship with Coreg and PJ.

"What are you thinking so hard about?"

Lettie walked in. The other woman had been visiting with Tegrig and Honrig at the park that was on the edge of town. It was a safe place with vegetation that boasted flowers and a large pond where funny looking birds swam. Some looked like a cross between a fish and a duck.

"Coreg is going back to the ship to bring back more of our things."

"Wow. That's great! I hope he finds some of my stuff. I miss having my parents' pictures."

"Mostly they are going to grab what they can from the hold of the ship. Did you have any pictures in what you had packed?" Andrea asked.

"Yeah, my favorite was in my quarters, but I doubt they can even get there." Lettie sighed. "Do you miss your family much?"

Andrea thought about it. "Some. I should miss them more, but I know it's useless. I'll never see them again. More than likely the Earth fell apart already and my brother is on some other planet trying to survive. There's nothing I can do about any of it."

"I know you're right, but I still miss them. They were great parents. They did everything they could to get me on the ship, so I'd have a chance at surviving."

Andrea nodded at the other woman. "It sounds like they loved you very much. Hold on to that. Not all the women here had a good home life like you and I did."

"I guess I didn't think of that," Lettie said. "I don't think Cindy Grenada did. She's gotten over her injuries, but she's very quiet and doesn't talk much about her past."

"You've been a good friend to her. I'm sure she appreciates it," Andrea said.

"What about you and Coreg and PJ? Is everything going okay between the three of you?" Lettie asked.

"Yes, it is. Other than this trip Coreg is going on. I don't want him to go, but I understand that he wants to help. I'll get over it."

"Don't stay mad at him, Andrea. He's totally gone on you. I've never seen a man look at someone like he looks at you. Well, I guess I see it in Della and Caro's men, but the way Coreg looks at you is as if you hung the moon in his eyes. PJ is in love with you for sure. He's always watching you with those sappy puppy dog eyes of his."

"Puppy dog eyes?" Andrea laughed. "I hadn't thought of him having those."

It pleased her that Lettie thought the men loved her. It went a long way to convincing her to tell them that she loved them as well. Maybe soon. First, they had to get over the hurdle of making love.

The two men walked back in twenty minutes later laughing about something. Andrea looked up from the dress she was hemming.

"What's so funny?" she asked.

"Deiog is attempting to make toys for the young we are all expecting. So far, they are not going well. He's using our history tapes to go by," Coreg told her.

"Maybe some of the men from Earth can give him some pointers," Andrea suggested.

"That's what we've been doing. He's exasperated right now." PJ chuckled.

"Maybe if he started with small things like simple blocks with letters painted on them, he can graduate up to something easier."

"The blocks are a good idea," Coreg said. "But, we use different symbols than your human alphabet, and the human males are arguing about that."

"I see." Andrea thought it was funny. "Well, it will be a while before they can play with toys anyway. Right now, they will only need soft things that are not dangerous to them."

"That is what PJ told them. The males who make our clothes are working on small dolls as you call them. Plus, one of our other males is working on safe products for teething and chewing for the young."

"Great idea. I think that if you can find the crates that there are a lot of baby things on the ship since we were supposed to have babies pretty soon after we landed. They thought of what we would need to begin with."

"I will look out for that. One of your unattached males is going with us. I hadn't realized that. The Major John Lance is going to help us find what we are seeking. It will go a long way to cutting down the time we will be out there."

"I'm glad he's settled down now. He was against our women from settling down with any of the Levassians," PJ said. "Now he's more relaxed and admits that he was jealous since there were so few women, and his had died during the crash."

"Some of the human males have come to terms that they might not end up with a woman of their own, and are spending more time working," Coreg added.

"I feel sorry for any man who ends up without a woman to make them happy. I wish there had been more of us to survive," Lettie added.

"I hope there won't be any fighting when the last of our women settle down. That would be so sad." Andrea set the dress aside. "I'm going to work on supper. Any requests?"

"Anything you make will be fine with me," Coreg said.

"I'll help. I want to talk to you." Lettie followed Andrea into the kitchen.

"What is it? You seem a little jumpy." Andrea pulled out a meal package from the food unit.

"I want to settle down with Tegrig and Honrig, but wanted to know what you thought about it."

"Do you care about them? Not just like them, but really care about them?"

"I do. They are so good to me and haven't rushed me or anything. I feel like it's time."

"Lettie, only you can answer that. I like the two men and how they treat you. If you want to settle down with them, I'm happy for you."

Andrea was happy for Lettie but worried that the woman was so young. Should she wait and see if someone else caught her eye, or go ahead and form a family unit with the two men now? She couldn't make that decision for the other woman.

"Thanks, Andrea. I was scared you'd insist that I wait. I'm going to wait a few more weeks before I make the decision. They aren't pressuring me or anything. They've said to take all the time I need, that they aren't going anywhere."

"That's good. Let it settle in with you before you give them a final answer. You might think of other things you need to talk about in the meantime." Andrea thought it was very adult of the other woman.

Maybe she wasn't giving Lettie enough credit for knowing what to do with her life. She'd seen her as young and naïve instead of a young woman who'd boarded a spaceship bound for a distant planet not knowing what to expect. Lettie had a good head on her shoulders. She'd make the right decision, and regardless of what she decided, Andrea would be there to talk when she needed to.

"Are you upset about Coreg going on the trip to get more stuff off the ship?" Lettie seemed to pick up on Andrea's unease.

"Yeah, but I can't be mad at him. He's only doing what he thinks is the right thing, and I admire him for suggesting it to the council to allow it."

"I know a lot of the other women here will be really thankful to have more of their things. It's one thing to end up on a strange planet, but it's altogether different to land somewhere without anything to remind you of home." Lettie touched on what Andrea had been thinking herself.

"I know that having my sewing machine really made me happy and has helped me settle down more with living on Levasso. Without it, I think I'd have gotten depressed pretty fast."

"See, your Coreg is going to help make it easier for everyone to be more comfortable living here." Lettie hugged Andrea before taking one of the bowls she'd filled over to the table.

Andrea sighed. The other woman was right. She needed to let it go and try not to worry about Coreg. Her anxiety would bleed over to him and he needed his head on the trip and not on her.

"Supper's ready guys," Lettie called out.

They talked during the meal about what was going on around the city. Coreg shared the council's take on several things, including females working outside the home. It seemed they were loosening some of the restrictions in order to make the women happier. Andrea thought they were wise after all, instead of restrictive men who knew nothing about them. It just took some time.

"I'd like to work at one of the health clinics," Lettie said. "I'd planned to go to nursing school before everything happened like it did back on Earth."

"That is something I'm sure they would allow since you wouldn't be in any danger," Coreg said. "Most of what they don't want is anything that will put a female in danger. They are very supportive and proud of your sewing, Andrea. They think you've found a niche and the fact that you're happy has gone a long way to lightening their beliefs about women working."

"I'm glad. Our women are used to contributing to society. There will probably be a few who just want to keep house and care for the children, but some will want more. Oh, and there are some who will want to be educators for when the children grow old enough to learn in school."

"That will be another discussion with the council," Coreg said with a sigh.

"Why do you say that?" Lettie asked.

"They will of course want them to learn all about Levasso and the Carrdine Galaxy as their home. Plus, they will need to learn our way of life since it is now yours. I can foresee that your people will want them to learn your life and language as well. I'm not sure how that will all work together." Coreg looked over at PJ.

PJ shrugged. "Children learn best at an early age. On Earth, most young children were taught a second language along with the English they learned. They pick up on languages and other skills easily when young. Some preschools taught them both languages at the ages of four and five."

"That should be communicated to the council once it becomes an issue. I supposed we have two or three years before it will become necessary to do so," Coreg said.

"I wonder what the babies will be like?" Lettie said.

"There's no way to tell until they are born. I know their health checks have been fine and the expecting females are in excellent health," Coreg told them.

"Are they going to be bigger than normal?" Lettie asked, looking over at Andrea with concern in her eyes.

"Yes, they will be some larger but not too large for them to deliver. If for some reason they have difficulty, their health leaders will remove the babies from them so they are not harmed in any way." Coreg passed the bowl of vegetables to Andrea.

Lettie looked confused. "I thought they were called healers."

"They are, but the senior healers are our health leaders," Coreg told her.

"So, they know about C-sections. Good. I wondered if that was ever performed here," Andrea said.

"But there haven't been any babies born here in a long time. What about the health leaders? Have they ever performed one before?" Lettie asked with wide eyes.

"Um, I suppose not, but they have probably done countless simulations since the females announced they were carrying young. Believe me, they are prepared for every possible situation," Coreg assured her.

"Don't worry so, Lettie. You are not even pregnant. They will have a lot of practice taking care of us by then." Andrea was reassuring herself as much as Lettie.

The idea that they hadn't taken care of a pregnant woman or a baby scared her. She was sure that Lettie, being so young, would be frightened. Especially when she was contemplating becoming a family unit with Tegrig and Honrig. Andrea wondered if that thought would color her decision on whether to agree to joining them now or not. She wouldn't blame the girl if she changed her mind.

Andrea thought about what that meant for her. Once they started becoming intimate to the point of having actual sex, her chances of becoming pregnant were great. Of course, the physicians, or health leaders as they put it, would have some experience by then if she did. Was she okay with that? Well, if she was going to have sex she'd have to be. And Andrea knew that time was growing closer. She couldn't expect the men to go without forever while they shared a bed.

"What are you looking so concerned about?" PJ asked.

"Just thinking about how Caro and Della might be feeling about being guinea pigs," she lied.

"What are guinea pigs and why do you say the females are those?" Coreg asked.

PJ laughed. "Guinea pigs are like being experiments. Caro and Della are the first women to have babies here on Levasso, so their deliveries will be experimental to your physicians or health leaders as you call them."

"Oh, well, I suppose that is true, but their health is of the utmost importance to all of Levasso. Nothing will be spared to keep them safe and healthy. We all want young playing in our city once more." Coreg smiled and patted Andrea's hand. "Do not worry so, little one."

Andrea narrowed her eyes at him. "It's kind of hard not to be a little worried when you're trusting your life and the life of your baby to men who've never delivered one before. It's pretty scary if you ask me."

"I've delivered a baby before," PJ told her.

"You never told me that," Andrea said. "When, where?"

"When I was with the volunteer fire department where I lived. We were called out along with the ambulance when a woman went into labor at home. She lived out in the country and we got there first." PJ smiled. "I got to catch the baby. It was awesome."

"See, little one. If you go into labor as he calls it, you will have us to help you. PJ knows how to catch a baby, whatever that means." Coreg grinned at her.

Everyone chuckled except Andrea. She narrowed her eyes at PJ. Evidently, he got the message because he smothered his laugh. It did make her feel a bit better that he'd actually attended a birth before in case she had a baby at home. As long as he was there to 'catch the baby', she'd be fine.

While everyone finished up the meal and Lettie helped her with the dishes, Andrea prepared herself for the coming night. Somewhere between when Coreg had told her about going on the trip the next morning and their discussion about having babies, she'd decided that tonight was the night they'd consummate their relationship. She wanted to before Coreg left when something could happen to him. It would give him an added reason to be extra careful.

Or so she hoped.

Chapter Ten

Andrea took her time preparing for bed. She'd managed to get them to let her go last this time when normally they insisted that she go first. She made sure she was clean-shaven and applied some of the scented body lotion Coreg had brought her from the ship the first time he'd gone. The gown she wore for sleeping in was their favorite color of pink. She didn't plan on wearing it for long.

Nerves flitted along her skin like tiny bursts of electricity, much like the bouncing balls in her stomach. It shouldn't be so hard to initiate intimacy with her men. Why was she this nervous? It wasn't like she was a virgin, just with them.

When she walked out of the bathroom, she found both men already in bed talking about the next morning. They immediately stopped talking as if believing it would upset her. Well, they were right, but she wouldn't let them know it. Instead, Andrea crawled up from the foot of the bed and scooted beneath the covers that the guys held up for her.

"Mmm, you smell delicious, PJ said.

"Yes, she does," Coreg added.

Both men leaned in closer and inhaled. It settled her nerves when she hadn't thought anything could. They wanted her. That was all that mattered.

"Are you going to kiss me?" she asked.

"Absolutely." PJ leaned in and took her lips.

Andrea wrapped her arms around his neck and held on while he plundered her mouth with his tongue. He mapped every inch of her mouth before sucking on her tongue until she entered his mouth to taste him as well. When he pulled back, there was heat in his eyes. Heat, that when she turned to Coreg, seemed to be mirrored in his.

She didn't have to ask, all it took was for her to lift her arms to his shoulders and he pounced. Where PJ had been demanding, Coreg was questioning with his exploration of her mouth with his. He thrust his tongue in and out before licking along hers. She hummed into his so that he pulled her tighter against his body.

The man was very happy to have her so close to him. She could feel his stiff dick pressing against her body. He felt huge to her. Then PJ cuddled up to her from behind, and his hard cock rubbed against her ass. They both were super aroused. Andrea wasn't sure they'd fit. She'd never been with a man as well-endowed as the two men in her life were.

"God, you smell so damn good. I can't wait to taste you again, Andrea." PJ's words near her ear seemed just for her.

Coreg pulled back and stared deep into her eyes. "Are you saying you're ready to become intimate, little one?"

"Yes."

She didn't get another word out as he pounced on her, nibbling along her jawline then down her neck to her shoulder. He nudged the gown aside to lick and suck at her shoulder.

"Take the gown off," PJ said.

"I will take care of it." Coreg backed away and shoved his hands beneath the covers to grab the gown and pull it over her head.

Andrea had to lift her hips so that he could pull it out from under her, then lift her arms over her head when he pulled up then off. She started to cover her breasts, but one look at Coreg's eyes had her stopping mid-motion. The silver of his eyes had darkened to a deep gray. She'd never seen them quite so dark before. He lifted a hand to touch them, almost reverently.

She looked over at PJ, who'd sat back slightly and waited as if letting Coreg have his moment. He knew this was a first for the other man. He'd never been with a woman before, and had never touched a woman's breasts.

"So soft and perfect," Coreg whispered. "Will you let me lick them, Andrea?"

"You can do anything you want to with them, Coreg. You and PJ can touch me anywhere," she said, a bit breathless by the combined looks of need in both men's eyes.

"You're so beautiful, little one." Coreg lowered his head and licked across her nipple.

Andrea couldn't help but moan at the gentle touch of his tongue. She arched toward him almost without thought. She wanted more. She needed to feel both of them touching her.

As if understanding her need, PJ molded one breast in his hand and covered as much as he could with his mouth, then he pulled back and sucked on just the nipple. Coreg took his lead to do the same. When he sucked on her nipple alongside PJ, Andrea nearly came instantly. Two mouths on her at one time were almost too much. She groaned and writhed between them. It felt so good, so right.

"She's perfect, PJ. How did I ever get so blessed to have her in my life?"

"She's a special woman, Coreg. I for one, will do everything I can to make her happy."

Andrea ran her hands through PJ's hair and tugged on Coreg's braid as they ravished her breasts. She could tell that her pussy was wet. It fluttered as if aching for something to fill it. She prayed they would do that soon. Her body was primed, all ready to come. She knew both men were amazing with their mouths, but she needed more than oral sex. She wanted their cocks inside of her.

"Please. I need you. I need you both. Don't play with me." Andrea pulled at their hair to get them off her breasts. "You can play with them later. They aren't going anywhere."

PJ chuckled. "I should hope not. What do you want, babe?"

"One of you inside of me. I'm desperate," she admitted.

"Coreg, she needs you, man. I have her mouth this time. I've been dying to have her mouth on my dick."

"I've heard of this but have never experienced it," Coreg said.

"You can watch if you have the energy once you're inside of her. Believe me, you won't be able to think about anything else, much less watch me."

"You are sure you are ready for me, little one?"

Andrea took his hand in hers then slid it down her abdomen to her sopping wet pussy. His eyes grew dark once more.

"Does it feel as if I'm ready for you, Coreg?"

"You're so wet. That is good. It will help me enter you."

"Less talk and more action," Andrea said.

PJ chuckled. "Better get to it."

Coreg climbed over her, dwarfing her as he did. She'd almost forgotten how tall he was until he stood on all fours staring down at her. She wasn't sure how she'd be able to take care of PJ with his head over hers nearly touching the headboard. Then he lifted her legs and sat back with one of her legs over an arm and the other hand grasping his cock. He pumped the shaft a few times as if testing his readiness, then rubbed the head of it against her slick opening.

"I wanted to taste you again, little one, but you are not giving me the chance."

"Next time, Coreg. I need you too much this time," she said.

Coreg slowly entered her, seeming to split her pussy open with his broad cock. Andrea could only thank God that she was so wet. He stretched her almost more than she could handle as he pushed in then pulled out slightly, only to delve deeper with each thrust of his dick. Andrea moaned as he moved in and out of her hot cunt. He'd entered her as far as he could go, bottoming out at her cervix before fully seating himself inside of her.

"Great gods. I never knew it would feel this good. She's like a hot, wet fist squeezing my cock," Coreg said between clenched teeth. "I will not last long. I'm already so close to my completion."

"Told you," PJ said.

While Coreg had been breaching her body, PJ had been rubbing his dick against her lips until she'd opened them for him. Now he was slowly pumping in and out of her mouth. She rubbed the bottom of his cock with her tongue as he entered her then retreated. Andrea couldn't believe that they were actually doing it. They were consummating their relationship, sealing their destiny. It felt right. Perfect.

PJ started increasing his pace even as Coreg pounded in and out of her with her legs over his arms. She felt her climax just out of reach as the two men tunneled in and out of her body. Coreg began to lose control, bumping against her cervix as he did. That little bite of pain was all she needed to climax. Her orgasm took her screaming around PJ's cock. He groaned and emptied his load in her mouth even as Coreg held still deep inside of her with his release.

When PJ pulled back, it was to collapse against the headboard. Coreg didn't move, he just knelt between her legs with his softening dick still deep inside of her. His eyes were closed, and his head thrown back. He looked like the statue of a satisfied man.

"Coreg? Are you okay?" Andrea finally asked.

"I'm in the heavens, little one." He dropped his head, drawing in long deep breaths of air. "It is so much more than I could ever have imagined. How have you not pounced on our Andrea before now, PJ?"

"The other man laughed. "Because I knew better. Never assume a woman wants sex until she lets you know she's ready to take that step. You could have certain delicate parts harmed if you try it."

"I see." Coreg slowly withdrew from her and laid next to her. "Thank you, little one. That was beyond anything I could have asked for. I will treasure you always and do whatever it takes to keep you happy."

PJ curled up next to her. "Do you need to get up yet?"

Coreg's brows furrowed. "She would leave us now?"

"No. But she might want to freshen up after our lovemaking," PJ explained.

"Ah. I see. I believe I even sweated on her," Coreg said. "I'm sorry, Andrea."

Andrea couldn't prevent a soft chuckle at his admission. "It's okay. There will be lots of that when we make love. I'm sweating as well. Thank you both for the orgasm. I wasn't sure I would come this first time together. I was so nervous and anxious about it."

"We'll always take care of you, babe. Need help getting up?" PJ asked.

She shook her head before crawling down the bed and stepping off at the foot to brush her teeth and do a little cleanup. She paused in the cleansing unit to think about the night. They'd more than taken care of her. They'd been careful of her. Though Coreg had bumped her cervix several times, she could tell he was trying not to hurt her. It had actually felt pretty good in a slightly painful sort of way. It had been the reason she'd climaxed in the end.

Now as she looked at herself in the mirror, Andrea drew in a deep breath and relaxed. Sleeping between the two men wouldn't be nearly as uncomfortable now that they'd made love. Where before she'd been anxious that they were uncomfortable with their obvious hard-ons, now she knew they were satisfied and could rest without being so aroused.

Just before she walked out of the unit and closed it up once again, she thought about the fact that she might become pregnant now that they'd begun to have sex. Was she okay with that? Well, she better be. There was no birth control on Levasso. She doubted they would look for a way to prevent pregnancies as long as there was a shortage of people on the planet. If they cherished children as much as she did, then she wouldn't mind having several of them. How many? She guessed that would depend on how much help she had raising them. Children were work, though they were a chore most women enjoyed.

Would her men want to help or expect her to handle all of that part of their lives? She expected that Coreg especially, would want to have a hand in raising them. They seemed starved for the chance to have children. Would PJ be the same way?

It would take time before she knew the answers to those questions. Even if she became pregnant, it would be between seven and nine months before she'd find out.

* * * *

Early the next morning, PJ woke Andrea so that she could see Coreg off. The other man had already gotten ready and was waiting on her in the communal living area. She rubbed the sleep from her eyes and pulled on one of the overly large dresses she used as a housecoat instead of the shift it was supposed to have been.

Coreg stood with a pack on his back at the door. His smile brightened his face when she threw herself into his arms.

"Please, please be careful, Coreg. I'm going to worry about you so remember to watch out for everything." Andrea hugged him fiercely.

"I will be very careful just for you, little one. Last night alone will assure that I am very cautious. I wish to come home to your arms."

"I'm holding you to that. Don't worry about anything here. We will be fine. Just concentrate on getting to and from the ship safely." Andrea tightened her hold before finally releasing him and taking a step back.

"Take care, Coreg. We'll be watching for you at sundown." PJ nodded at the other man.

Andrea watched as the other part of her family unit walked through the door to disappear out into the still dark early morning. She knew they would wait until first light at the city's gate, then drive through with three transports. She knew Coreg would be on one of them and prayed that they would all return safely.

"Don't worry, babe. Coreg will be fine. There are three soldiers experienced in the jungle going with them. They won't let anything happen to the others, especially Coreg."

"Why especially him?" she asked.

"Because he's in a family unit now, and they don't want you upset or unhappy. Keeping him alive is tantamount to assuring your happiness." PJ pulled her into a hug. "Come on. It's too early to be up. Let's go back to bed and rest a little longer. I'm still beat from last night."

Andrea smiled when he winked at her. He was just trying to cheer her up, but she appreciated it. PJ was good about that. He had always understood her moods and seemed to know what to do or say to make her feel better. It was why she'd taken to him when she hadn't her other partner. She was sorry that he was dead, but she liked to believe that everything happened for a reason.

"I'm going to get something to drink and be right there," Andrea said.

"Don't be long or I'll come looking for you. No sewing yet." PJ wagged his finger at her like a scolding mother.

She couldn't help but smile at him before he turned and walked down the hall toward their sleeping chamber. She continued into the meal prep area and programmed a cold drink. She sipped the cool liquid while she thought about the night before. They'd all three come at the same time. It was amazing and a little scary at the same time. She was part of a family now. It wasn't just about her, but about them.

When she returned to the sleeping chamber, would PJ want to make love without Coreg there with them? How was she supposed to handle that? Surely they didn't always have to be together before having sex. Would one of them get upset with the other one if she made love with the other one?

Andrea sighed. She couldn't worry about that. It would drive her insane to always wonder what the other would think or how they would feel. She just needed to worry about them as a family and what was good for the family. The sex would take care of itself, and if PJ was to be believed, the two of them would work out any differences without involving her. Everything else included her in the decision.

She set the empty glass in the sink and strode from the room and down the hall to where PJ waited for her. She found him snoring on his side of the bed. Yeah, he'd been beat all right. She smothered a laugh as she climbed into bed to snuggle next to one of her men.

Chapter Eleven

Coreg breathed a sigh of relief when they made it to the ship without incident. They entered the opening in the hull and spread out to locate the containers housing personal effects, using the information that both PJ and Major Lance had given them. Coreg boxed up all of Andrea's things and stacked the boxes on one of the hover crafts they would use to carry what they found back to their transports, and then back home.

He continued looking until he found the container with Lettie's things and did the same for her. He was content now that he'd found their things. One of the others was tasked with finding whatever they could of Della and Caro's stuff. He was now looking for any container that might have things for young in them. The humans called them infants and babies. It wasn't a term he was used to, but he searched for any indication of these items on the listings outside the containers.

Finally, he located two large crates labeled child and baby. He called over one of the other males to help him open the containers. Inside, they found exactly what they were looking for. It took he and the other male another hour to box them up and load them into one of the hover crafts.

They spent over six hours loading belongings on the crafts before the lead soldier announced it was time to return. It would take another couple of hours to reach the transports, then at least an hour back to the city by the time they reloaded the hover crafts on the transports.

Coreg was proud of their success in locating so much of what they'd come after. He couldn't wait to see his Andrea's face when she saw the rest of her things. Even Lettie's smile would be welcome. He knew she was hoping they'd locate hers as well.

"Coreg. Watch out."

Just as he looked up, one of the soldiers knocked him down just as an aragus jumped at him. The soldier took the brunt of the attack, but Coreg could feel the blood running down his arm. He rolled away from the huge creature then took the knife he always kept in his boot out and jumped on the thing's back to get it to let go of his rescuer.

The soldier managed to crawl away while the creature tried to get Coreg off its back. Coreg drove his knife under the armor-like skin, trying to hit something lethal on the creature. From the way it screamed, he hoped he was succeeding. He was afraid that killing it would be the only way he would be able to get off of it alive.

The other two soldiers raced to the fight, one pulling the other soldier back to the hover crafts for the other males to take care, then joining his partner to attack the aragus. They yelled instructions to Coreg on how to disable the creature while they used every chance they got to wound it.

Finally, he managed to get a vital organ and the aragus collapsed. It was still alive, but no longer fighting them. He slipped off its back and all but crawled away from the dreaded creature. The soldiers dispatched the fallen animal then returned to help the others bandage up their colleague and Coreg. His arm hurt worse than anything he'd ever felt before, but he'd survived and would return to his Andrea. The soldiers had congratulated him on defeating an aragus, even though he pointed out that he'd had their help. They were impressed nonetheless that he'd jumped on the thing's back to save their friend.

"You would have done the same. I couldn't let the thing harm another male. We have much to be happy about now. Soon there will be young, and more of us need to know how to protect our greatest assets," he told them.

"We will make sure everyone knows that you are an aragus killer," one of the males said.

"I'm not sure that is a good idea. My female is going to be very unhappy with me," he told them.

"Why? You were a strong male and a hero," one of the other males asked.

"Because I promised not to get hurt. She will be worried that I have been injured." Coreg hoped that she would be so happy that he'd returned and brought her things that she would overlook his slight injury.

He winced, well, it wasn't exactly slight. It would mean he would be off work for a few weeks from the looks of it. He was sure he had a broken bone as well as the cuts from the thing's teeth. No, she would be quite angry with him before she forgave him.

Oddly enough, he was fine with that. It meant she cared for him and that he had a female to care about him. He was truly blessed among Levsassians to have a female in a family unit. The fact that he shared her with PJ was nothing to him. It meant that if something had happened to him, PJ would be there to care for her in his absence. He valued his new friend for that. He hoped PJ thought the same thing concerning him. They would talk once he finished begging his female's forgiveness.

No sooner than they entered the gates of the city, word spread about their adventures. He and the wounded soldier were whisked to the healer's before he could stop to let his family know that he was fine. He asked to use a communication unit to let them know he was home, but the healer refused until they'd scanned and treated him.

Once they'd set his arm and repaired the lacerations, Coreg commandeered a communication unit and called his home. The fact that no one answered worried him. What was wrong that they weren't there waiting on him?

He soon found out when a frantic Andrea burst into the room where he waited for the sealant to cure on his injuries, followed by a very unhappy PJ. She threw herself at him, hugging him to the point of pain despite the pain medicine they'd injected him with. She looked him over as if assuring herself he was truly all right. Then she crossed her arms and glared at him.

"If you weren't already injured, I'd kill you myself."

"I don't understand?" Coreg began.

"You promised you wouldn't get hurt. They are talking all over the city about how brave you were saving one of the soldiers from an aragus. They are the trained ones, not you. What were you thinking?" Andrea shook her head, her eyes bright with unshed tears. "You could have been killed, Coreg."

"The soldier saved my life first, little one. I couldn't lay there while he was seriously injured or killed after he risked his life to take the full brunt of the creature's wrath. I didn't think, I just reacted." Coreg sighed when she just shook her head, allowing a single tear to slide down her cheek.

"Not good enough. You can't scare me like this. You aren't a soldier. You're my male," she said.

"PJ. Help me here. I can't stand to see her so unhappy. She's shedding tears. This is terrible." Coreg stood up, wincing at the pain that radiated down his injured arm.

"Don't get up." Andrea shoved him back down on the table. "Not until the healer lets you leave. Then you're coming home with us."

"I'm sorry, Coreg, but she's the boss when it comes to times like this. I was lucky to keep up with her when she heard that you'd been injured. Then, when they started talking about how you were a hero, she just about lost me getting here. The woman can run." PJ shrugged.

"I'm fine, little one. Please do not cry. I will make it up to you. I found the rest of your things, and I even brought back Lettie's things," he told her.

"I don't care about our things when it meant that you were hurt. Nothing is worth you or PJ to me. I love you. I can't stand the idea that something nearly happened to you, Coreg."

"You love me?" Coreg focused on that one thought.

She loved him.

"I love you both. I've wanted to say it for a while now, but wanted the time to be perfect. Now I wish I'd already told you. What if you'd been killed and I hadn't said the words? It would have broken me. Now do you see why you can't do this again?" she asked.

"Do not worry, Andrea. I won't be going again. Now that we have your things and the baby things for the young, I will remain here working and by your side. I am truly sorry that I scared you." Coreg reached out with his good arm to take her hand in his. He held it to his heart. "I love you as well, little one. With all my heart."

Andrea smiled up at him through teary eyes. He loved that smile but without the tears. He wanted to see that smile all the time.

PJ wrapped his arms around their Andrea from behind and rested his chin on her head. She reached up and cupped his cheek in her hand.

"I love you, too, silly. You both mean the world to me. I don't want my world to ever be without the two of you in it," she said.

"I love you as well, babe. You're what makes our family unit a family. Nothing matters more than your happiness. Coreg won't be going anywhere again. Neither will I. We've got jobs here and don't need to go back to the ship. We'll leave that to the soldiers and other men." PJ caught Coreg's gaze and lifted his chin. "Right, Coreg?"

"That is correct." He smiled at the other male. "I also found your things and packed them away with Andrea's. They should deliver the boxes by in the morning," he said.

"Thanks. I'm glad you found them, but if you hadn't there wouldn't have been anything I couldn't live without. I have everything I need right here in this room." PJ pulled Andrea into his arms and clasped Coreg on his uninjured arm.

* * * *

Andrea couldn't stop looking at Coreg on the trip back to their home. They'd taken a transport to lessen the effort on Coreg by walking back with his injuries. She could have lost him, nearly had. She didn't think she was going to be able to rest easy for a long time. Nearly losing him had sealed her need for both of them to always be there in her life.

"What are you thinking so hard about, babe? I can almost see the wheels working in your head." PJ took one of her hands in his. Andrea held fast to Coreg's as well.

"Just trying to get past nearly losing Coreg. It's going to be awhile before I'm going to sleep easy."

"Little one, I'm fine. Please don't fret on my account. Nothing is going to happen to either of us. We will return to our normal duties soon enough. There's nothing dangerous about overseeing the fields or working on the broken machinery that PJ does. Your fears are unfounded.

"Don't tell me not to worry about you guys. I'm going to do it regardless. You're getting hurt nearly paralyzed me. I was so scared of what I was going to find when we got to the health clinic, that I nearly threw up." Andrea squeezed his hand. "I'm going to worry about you. I can't help it."

"I am sorry I worried you so, little one. I will do my best not to allow that to happen again." Coreg smiled down at her.

Andrea loved his smile. His silvery eyes brightened and the way his lips curled up reminded her of a statue back home, no, back on Earth. It had always intrigued her. Coreg was a handsome man with his silver skin and bright eyes. He was strong with muscles like all Levassians. She knew he worked hard, though he was a supervisor of sorts. She knew PJ worked hard since he handled heavy machinery trying to make it work. Of the two jobs, PJ's probably posed the greatest risk.

"Both of you must promise me to be very careful. I don't think I can handle another injury between the two of you. Promise?" she asked.

"We promise, babe. No taking risks. Neither of us wants to worry you," PJ said.

"When we are home, I want you to go straight to bed, Coreg. You need to rest so that you heal. No arguing with me. I'll bring you something to eat there." Andrea knew he'd resist but was ready for him.

"I do not need to rest in bed. I can rest in the living area so I can be close to you," Coreg complained.

"If you're doing better in the morning, you can sit in the living area while I sew. I can keep an eye on you that way." Andrea shook a finger at him.

Coreg looked over at PJ with a look that Andrea interpreted to be entreaty to appeal to their woman to show leniency. She shot a sharp look PJ's way. He better not take Coreg's side.

"Sorry, buddy, but I have to live with her, too. You're confined to bed tonight," he said. "Look on the bright side. It's almost time to go to bed anyway. Enjoy the meal in bed. It's considered a rare treat on Earth."

"Eating in bed is a treat? That doesn't make sense." Coreg frowned.

"I'll explain later. Just go with it for now. It makes our woman happy." PJ winked at the other man.

Andrea watched their byplay with amusement, then it hit her again that Coreg had come near to dying and she sobered. Nothing in that ship had been worth his life to her.

They pulled up outside their home. Andrea insisted on helping him out of the transport and into the house. On one level, she knew she couldn't support his weight should he falter, and PJ would have been the better choice, but on the other hand, it made her feel good to help him into their home.

"Let's get you out of the rest of your clothes and into bed. You're not going to be able to use your left hand to do it." Andrea followed him into the bedroom.

She could hear PJ talking to Lettie, apprising her of Coreg's condition and no doubt letting her know that Andrea was going off the deep end about it. She didn't care. At least for tonight she would be in some form of control over Coreg's care. She needed that control when she'd been helpless when he'd been injured back in the jungle.

Once she had Coreg tucked safely in bed, she returned to the living area to talk to Lettie about finishing their meal. The other woman had already done so.

"Thank you, Lettie. I'm not sure I would have been able to cook without burning something," Andrea said.

"I didn't mind. I'm so glad Coreg wasn't seriously injured. I know you're sick over it."

"I could have lost him, Lettie. I don't know what I would have done."

"Well, you didn't. Don't torture him over it. I'm sure he was a little upset about it as well. He faced an aragus for goodness sake. We all know how dangerous that is, even for the trained soldiers. He's considered a hero now. He saved one of the soldiers after that soldier threw himself between the aragus and Coreg. Few Levassians would have done that. They say they would have frozen in place out of fear." Lettie pulled Andrea into a hug.

"I don't care that he was a hero. All I care about is that he was hurt and I could have lost him. I won't fuss at him anymore though. He did what needed to be done. I can't argue with that, but I'm still shaking inside over it."

"Take a deep breath and carry his meal to him. If you feed it to him, he might see that supper in bed isn't so bad," Lettie told her with a wink.

Andrea smiled and drew in a deep breath before letting it out slowly. She would be fine once her gut stopped quivering like a bowl of Jell-O. She loaded up a plate with enough food to feed two then carried it into the bedroom on a tray. She sat the tray across Coreg's lap and proceeded to feet him from it.

"This is nice," he said. "Thank you, little one."

"Don't get used to it," she said chuckling. "It doesn't happen often."

"I'm humbled that you would feed me now. I understand it is a gift from you."

"It makes me feel better to do it. Now be quiet and eat all your vegetables."

"Maybe later I can eat you," Coreg said, his eyes growing dark.

"Much later. You're recuperating. We're not playing around while that arm is healing."

"I don't need my arm to pleasure you, Andrea. Just my mouth."

Heat burned up Andrea's neck and into her cheeks. How this man could make her blush when he was injured amazed her.

"Rest, Coreg. You'll be back on your feet soon enough. When you are, we'll make up for lost time.

"I can't wait."

Chapter Twelve

Andrea couldn't wait for Coreg and PJ to return home. Word had spread that Caro was in labor at the health clinic. It was only seven months, but they'd all been told that most Levassian infants were born at seven months. Since both of Caro's men were Levassian, it stood to reason that she might give birth earlier than a human couple. Still, she was anxious and wanted to be there to hear what was going on.

PJ arrived home first and hugged her when he heard the news.

"That's wonderful. As soon as Coreg gets here, we'll go and wait so we can welcome the new baby into the world."

"I can hardly believe it. Seven months seems too soon. I know they've been monitoring her and the baby, but seven months, PJ."

"Trust them that they know what they are doing. They have devices that are far more advanced than what we had back on Earth. They know if the baby is ready or not."

Coreg walked in with a huge smile on his face. "You've heard the news?" he asked.

"Yes. Hurry up both of you and get changed. I want to go to the health center," she said.

Coreg followed PJ to the sleeping chambers to change with Andrea following them.

"You do realize that all of Levastah is probably going to be there. We're all excited about this birth. It will be the first one in many, many years," Coreg said.

"I don't care. I want to go. Surely as a female I can get closer to see the baby once he's born." Andrea would use her revered status as much as she could in order to be close by.

"We shall see. I will try to get you close to the clinic," Coreg said.

Once the men had changed, the three of them hurried out the door and down the street, only to find a large crowd waiting outside the health center's doors. Andrea sighed. Coreg was right, there wouldn't be any way to get her inside the clinic. From the conversations around them, the only people allowed inside the clinic were the council and relatives. They'd also brought Della in just in case she went into labor since they'd conceived so close together.

"How long do Levassian's usually go through labor?" she asked Coreg.

"I'm not sure. I don't remember from my childhood and never heard from anyone concerning it," Coreg told her.

They stood around talking with other Levassians while they waited to hear any news that might come out of the clinic. It did seem that most of the city had congregated in the streets to hear as soon as the birth was announced.

Two hours later, a health worker emerged through the doors and waved his hands to quiet the crowd.

"Mother Caro has just delivered a healthy boy. Both mother and young are well. The family thanks you for your support and hopes that you will return home as joyous as they are at this time. The young will be on display tomorrow afternoon once he's gone through all of his tests and has a good rest. You can file through the nursery to look through the window. Caro only asks that you don't tap on the window and upset the young." The man nodded and returned inside the clinic.

There were cheers and back slaps as everyone turned to return home. Andrea hugged both men and took their arms as they walked back to their home. She was relieved that both mother and child were healthy and happy. She hoped the labor hadn't been overly painful. They hadn't announced the infant's weight or length. That worried her a bit. Was he overly large or long? She couldn't wait to see him the next day.

"The city is going to be celebrating tomorrow. There will be food and excitement at the city's center commune. We should go and celebrate with everyone," Coreg said.

"It sounds like fun," PJ commented. "What do you think, babe?"

"Absolutely. We're a part of Levastah now. If they are celebrating the baby's birth, then we should do the same. I hope they do the same for Della's baby," she said.

"They will. They are the first of what we all hope will be many births." Coreg opened the door to their home then followed them inside.

"Where is Lettie?" Coreg asked.

"She's spending the evening with her beaus. She'll be in before long," Andrea told him.

"That leaves us some alone time," PJ said. "I'm thinking we should celebrate privately as well."

"Really." Andrea smiled up at both men. "What did you have in mind?"

"Driving you crazy with need, then making you scream our names," Coreg said.

"That sounds like fun." Andrea backed away from the two men then ran for the sleeping chambers.

She'd barely reached the door when Coreg snatched her up and turned her over his shoulder. She couldn't help but giggle as he carried her into the chamber and dropped her ass first on the bed. She giggled as she bounced then came to rest lying on her back.

PJ laughed and fell on her. He caged her in and kissed her, his mouth ravishing hers before he stopped and started pulling off her shirt. Coreg worked below, unfastening her skirt and sliding it down her body. Andrea giggled at their obvious hurry to remove her clothes. She couldn't wait for what was to come. She loved making love with them. They were both so attentive and generous.

"I'm the only one naked here. You better catch up or I'm going to start without you," she said.

When she pulled at her nipples with both hands then slid one hand down her abdomen to rest at her pussy, both men froze, staring at her hand with their mouths open. She slid one finger down her slit then back up to circle her clit. They groaned together as she once again slid her finger down then dipped inside her pussy before returning to her clit.

Coreg snapped out of the trance first and began to strip out of his clothes. PJ wasn't far behind him. They each crawled up the bed on either side of her and used their mouths to torture her breasts. Andrea squirmed between them as they sucked and nipped at her nipples. Coreg made his way down her body to kneel between her legs on the floor. He spread her legs and sighed.

"I love licking your sweet juices, little one. You taste like the saufass fruit we make our drinks from. Tart and sweet all at the same time." Coreg lowered his head and blew on her wet folds.

Andrea moaned.

PJ continued to torment her breasts using one hand and his mouth. She wanted them. She didn't need the foreplay, but she knew that once Coreg started working his magic between her legs, there was no stopping him until he was ready. He truly loved oral sex, both giving and getting. Though Andrea couldn't take all of him by any stretch of the imagination, she was able to suck enough of him that he came within minutes of her putting her mouth to his cock and balls.

Coreg ran his nose up her slit then breathed in before replacing it with his tongue. He stabbed her slit with it then lapped at her juices. When he began circling her clit, Andrea had to dig her fingers into the sheets to keep from screaming. It felt so damn good she didn't think she'd last long. The man could use his tongue like a weapon.

"Please, Coreg. I'm so close."

He chuckled against her pussy then stabbed one thick finger deep into her cunt while licking light circles around her bundle of nerves. He knew she needed more pressure there to climax, but he kept it almost feather-light as he drove her higher and higher with his fingers and mouth.

Finally, Coreg had pity on her and sucked hard on her clit. This took her to the top where she teetered before he nipped her clit and sent her spiraling over the top into an orgasm that threatened to make her pass out. Her scream seemed to spur him on so that he licked the tender nub until she pulled at his braid to get him to stop.

"Oh, God. I can't move after that," she finally said after catching her breath.

"We're not finished with you yet, babe," PJ said. "We want in that hot body. We're going to make you scream again."

"You'll kill me," she breathed out. "Coreg nearly did it with his mouth."

Coreg chuckled but climbed onto the bed and laid down next to her. He took her hand in his and brought it to his mouth where he laid a gentle kiss against her palm before closing it.

"You are perfect, little one."

"Look at Coreg's dick, babe. He's hard and stiff waiting on that hot little pussy of yours. Climb on him and ride him," PJ said.

Andrea smiled and rolled over to straddle Coreg's body. She grasped his thick cock with two hands and pumped him several times until he bucked beneath her and grabbed her by the shoulders.

"Take me, Andrea. I need to be inside of you."

She knelt over him then, with him guiding her by holding his dick still, she slowly slid down his thick shaft. She moved up then back down until he bumped her cervix, then she used her knees to support her. Coreg lifted her up and down with his hands on her hips. Each time he lifted her then let her slide back down on his shaft, Andrea felt as if he were in her throat. She squeezed him with her pussy, eliciting a curse from him.

"Easy, little one. You don't want me to come too soon." Coreg squeezed her hips.

"You feel so good inside of me. I'm full of your cock, Coreg." Andrea lifted with her thighs when Coreg pulled her off his shaft nearly all the way before letting her slide back down, her juices easing the way.

"PJ, you need to hurry. I'm not going to last long. She's so hot and tight. I'm going to come soon." Coreg threw back his head when she sank around him again.

"Lean forward, babe. I need to prepare you."

"Hurry, PJ. I'm so close. Coreg's cock is driving me crazy."

PJ chuckled. "I think it's you driving him crazy, babe."

With Andrea laying over Coreg's chest, PJ squeezed lube on her back hole then massaged it inside her ass. He added more lube and entered her with one finger, slowly pumping it in and out of her dark passage. She itched all over, needing something to make the itch go away. Somehow, Andrea knew that once PJ was in her ass, she'd go insane with the need to move. Right now, all she could do was lay there, waiting for PJ to finish prepping her for his cock.

PJ added more lube and a second finger. This pinched, seeming to burn her as he pumped the two digits in and out of her ass. She moaned as the burning sensation slowly turned into something more. More pleasure. More need.

"Please. Please," she moaned.

"Please what, babe? Tell me what you need." PJ continued to pump the two fingers in and out of her back hole.

"I need you inside me."

"Where? How, Andrea?" he asked.

"I need you to fuck me in my ass. Now!"

Andrea was done with the word games. She needed him inside of her to stop the itching need that was driving her insane. She knew that once he managed to get in her ass she'd be helpless to talk or breathe or anything. The pleasure would consume her and spit her out.

PJ removed his fingers then added more lube inside her hole before fitting his cockhead to her opening and slowly pressing inward. It hurt for a few seconds before he surged forward past the resistant rings and entered her to the hilt. He stopped, then slowly began to move with Coreg retreating when PJ thrust deeper. Then PJ withdrew while Coreg tunneled inside her tight, wet cunt.

Andrea could only moan as they pressed her between them. She let them move her as they wished, knowing she'd soon climax from their stuttering movements. The feel of PJ in her ass turned dark and hot. He stimulated nerve endings she'd never associated with pleasure before they'd begun to share her at the same time. Now she could feel her body grow closer and closer to an orgasm that would surely devastate her.

"I'm not going to be able to hold out much longer," Coreg bit out.

"Neither am I. She's so fucking hot and tight back here. Especially with you inside her pussy."

"Andrea, you've got to come, babe. We're losing it," PJ told her.

"I'm so close. Dear Lord, please don't leave me." Andrea panted as she grew closer to her climax.

PJ pulled her back so that Coreg could reach her clit. The other man lightly pinched it before surging up to hit her cervix. That was all it took for her to scream out her orgasm once more. This time, the scream was almost silent as the pleasure took her voice and her breath.

By the time she came to, both men had withdrawn from her and were gently stroking her skin. Had she passed out?

I guess I did. That was so hot. I think every time it gets better. If it keeps on, they'll kill me one day.

But what a way to go.

"You okay, little one?" Coreg asked.

"Yeah. I think so. You guys nearly killed me."

PJ chuckled. "You nearly killed us. When you climaxed, you clamped down on our dicks until we thought you'd pinch them off. I've never come so hard in my life, babe."

"Same here," she said with a laugh.

"Let's get you cleaned up, little one. Do you think you can stand to shower off?" Coreg asked.

"I think so. If I can't, I'm sure you can hold me up," she said.

The three of them stumbled into the cleansing chamber and squeezed into the shower that was made for two, but they'd managed to make it work for three. While Coreg held her up, PJ washed her off. Then Coreg cleaned up while PJ kept her standing. Once they were all washed and dried, they managed to make it back to the bed and slept like worn out children.

Just before Andrea fell asleep, she whispered, "I love you."

She was sure she heard it back.

Chapter Thirteen

Early the next morning, the three of them and Lettie hurried through their morning meal, then together with Honrig and Tegrig. They walked down to the health center to stand in line to view the baby. Andrea was super excited. She wanted to see what the new addition to Levastah looked like.

They stood in a slow-moving line for nearly an hour before finally making it to the window where the sleeping infant of Caro's lay behind the glass. He had lightly tanned skin and was large for a one-day old. Andrea winced at his size. She hoped Caro really was okay. The size of the baby would suggest she was sore at the very least.

She nodded to one of the health workers. "Can I visit Caro? Is she doing okay?"

"She's fine. There are no visitors right now. Perhaps tomorrow if you want to try again. She is resting between feedings."

"But she is okay, right?" Andrea asked again.

"She is. The birth went as planned and she held her young immediately afterward, along with her males. We are all joyous over this."

"I'm excited, too. The baby was rather large for us."

"He is a strong young and will do fine." The healthcare worker walked over to remind others not to tap on the glass, leaving Andrea to return to where her men were standing.

"The baby is amazing but really large for a newborn," she told them.

"I agree. That even makes me wince," PJ said.

"He is small to me. Though I've never seen a young just born, I've seen pictures of them and this little one is not average for us. I am sure that is best though since a human female had him." Coreg looked back at the window where more Levassians were huddled. "Have they picked out a name yet?"

"There wasn't one on the bed. Hopefully they will announce it before they go home. I want to see Caro tomorrow. The health worker said she might be receiving a few visitors then." Andrea looped her arms through Coreg's and PJ's as they walked back to their home.

"Are you worried about having a large baby, little one?" Coreg asked.

"Well, the size of that one was kind of shocking."

PJ chuckled. "If you go past seven months you'll know it is a human baby. If you go into labor at seven months, Coreg and I will hold your hands and let you squeeze them to your heart's desire."

"That's not all I'll be squeezing if I end up with as large a baby as Caro's. Hear me, Coreg?"

"I believe I might become celibate if you're talking about my genitalia, little one. I do not think that I would enjoy it if you squeezed me there more so than normal." Coreg moved a little away from her once they reached their home.

"Just don't put a bowling ball in my belly and we'll be fine," she told him.

PJ laughed, then sobered when Andrea looked his way. "Don't think you won't get the same treatment even if it is full human. You're a big man, too."

"Um, maybe we should think about this," PJ suggested.

"Are you saying no young, little one?" Coreg's face fell.

Andrea sighed. "No. I'm not saying no young. I'll have your babies, but remember that during labor I'm going to curse you to the ends of the Earth. Once it's over, I'll be too excited about the baby to remember all the pain. I'd tread carefully when I do get pregnant.

"We'll always tread carefully around you, babe. You're our woman and all we want to do is make you happy." PJ pulled her into his arms and kissed her. "I love you, babe. To the suns and back."

Coreg tugged her free of PJ's grasp. He kissed her as well." I love you, little one. More than a thousand hearts worth. You are my everything."

Andrea pulled both men close to her. "I love you both. You are my heart and soul. I never want to be without you both."

"Forever," all three of them said at the same time.

THE END

WWW.MARLAMONROE.COM

Siren Publishing, Inc.
www.SirenPublishing.com

CPSIA information can be obtained
at www.ICGtesting.com
Printed in the USA
LVOW10s1446100418

572940LV00030B/776/P